About the Author

Dr Steve Wooltorton resides in Cornwall. He has recently retired from a long career in medicine and remains an interested observer of the issues of the day. His hobbies include tennis and cliff top runs and walks along the Cornish coast.

Four Talks to the Women's Institute by William Vesuvius Smith

Dr Steve Wooltorton

Four Talks to the Women's Institute by William Vesuvius Smith

Olympia Publishers
London

www.olympiapublishers.com
OLYMPIA PAPERBACK EDITION

A CIP catalogue record for this title is available from the British Library.

ISBN: 978-1-80074-100-3

The characters in this book are fictitious, apart from national figures from past and present who are referred to. They are not supposed to represent any persons, living or dead. The locale is invented, even though it is situated somewhere in Cornwall.

First Published in 2022

Olympia Publishers
Tallis House
2 Tallis Street
London
EC4Y 0AB

Printed in Great Britain

Dedication

This book is dedicated to all those who look for and implement ideas which work for themselves, their country and mankind.

Acknowledgements

Bill Bryson. One Summer. America 1927. Chapter 12.
Neale Donald Walsch. Communion with God.

REFLECTIONS

William Vesuvius Smith found himself chuckling at the name his parents had bestowed upon him some seventy years ago. It was a good reflection of their own quirkiness and over the years, he had come to embrace and enjoy that side of their characters. They had always declared that most middle names were wasted on the fading memories of various relatives, when they should be used to inject a sense of excitement, fun and inspiration into a new person's life. It was a family thing. William had two cousins named in turn, Elizabeth Pacific and Rosemary Atlantic. With the belated arrival of another boy into William's family, volcanic leanings emerged again and the younger brother rejoiced in the name of Archibald Stromboli. Archie bore the tribulations of his initials stoically throughout his life.

As his friends gradually became aware of his middle name, the jokes remained similar. They were usually about William being about to erupt over something. It never became a nickname, partly because it didn't shorten easily and, also, William's own temperament was a calm one. Whilst working for Médecins sans Frontiere in war-torn Congo, where the hospital admissions were often dramatic and multiple, he was sometimes referred to as Dr Cool. This he took as a compliment, even though the truth may have been that since the language of the hospital was French, some of his coolness was possibly because he hadn't quite understood what was going on. His name of usage from school days onwards, was plain and simple Bill. The only exception to that came from his doting mother, to whom he was Billy in day-to-day life and William, spoken loudly, when he was in trouble.

Well, if there were times in the Congo when he was slow to pick up what was going on, then now, ten years later, he felt even more behind the pace and confused by what life in general was throwing up.

He was in a reflective mood, sitting in the beer garden of the local pub, The Red Lion. The dozen or so outside tables were only partly occupied and the pub behind him lay pleasantly bedecked in ivy and a pink, flowering, rambling rose. The scene was quintessentially English. Bill enjoyed things English, having spent many years far away from home. This was England at its rural best. He lived in a relatively far-flung outpost of England, at Tregannion, in Cornwall. The village was rapidly expanding in size and could now almost be described as a small town. It was near the centre of Cornwall but within reach of the sea, whose influence pervaded the whole county.

The sun warmed him and the breeze gently rustled the leaves behind. He first contemplated the bubbles appearing within his full glass of beer and watched them wobbling their way upwards to the surface, through the amber coloured Doom Bar bitter. There was no need to start drinking it yet.

That was another great name, Doom Bar. It was the name of a dangerous sand bar lying at the mouth of the River Camel estuary in Cornwall. Lives had been lost there as small boats ventured over the bar at high water, heading for the lock-protected haven of Padstow harbour. Bill, who had spent much of his life living in Cornwall, knew that there wasn't a decent harbour for small boats anywhere along the North Cornish coast. They were either narrow and tricky to enter, or empty at low water as the tide receded. He had once tried to rouse interest in building a small quay in Newquay Bay, close to the old lifeboat slip there. He put his idea out in the local newspaper. There was no local support for the idea forthcoming, just a lot of defensive calls to arms to protect the local bird and sea life from attack. He was surprised that the local boatmen hadn't responded. Bill had once found himself stuck off the north Cornish coast, alone in a small sailing boat. The wind had been a strong northerly. To Bill, it was a shame not to take advantage of the only piece of Cornish coastline that could be converted into an all-weather, all-tide refuge. Then, he surmised, most people had never had the experience of an uncomfortable night alone at sea, wishing there was a welcoming harbour to slide into. Most of them never would. He wondered if he would ever set out to sea again. He was getting a bit long in the tooth for strenuous activity.

His thoughts meandered onwards to his bodily state of health and his current, unresolved, daily problem of fatigue. His mental survey started at the top of his body and thought its way down.

He was comfortable with his bald head and had been for years. Once he realised, as a young man, that girls seemed indifferent to the loss of his locks, it ceased to worry him. The little that remained was still brown-coloured at first glance, especially when wet. Closer inspection revealed a lot of grey, which he described to his grown-up children as 'iron grey', when they laughed about it. His eyes depended totally on glasses for reading now. Distance vision remained passable and legal for driving, but the optician had told him cheerily that there were early cataracts in both eyes. For now, armed with his glasses which remained permanently with him either on his nose or in a holster on his belt, vision was not a problem. Neither was his hearing. Bill knew that deafness is noticed last by the sufferer but so far, there had been no complaints about an over-loud TV.

His teeth were, he thought, in reasonable shape — irregular but healthy. One mightily obvious defect was his missing right upper central incisor. This was cleverly hidden by a small plate which Bill hated. He couldn't wait to get a bridging job completed, but three days before the procedure was due to be finished, all the dentists throughout the country closed down due to the Covid-19 virus pandemic. He had lost the tooth due to a blow on the mouth from a random backfist strike whilst playing rugby for his school. The ball was a good thirty yards away when he was struck but tellingly, Bill never blamed the perpetrator of that wild strike. Instead, he blamed himself for not being quick enough to duck. He couldn't complain. The porcelain cap which initially replaced his damaged tooth had lasted fifty years — not bad, he reflected.

His face was a lined, friendly, lopsided affair. The lopsidedness was because his spine was slightly crooked and the muscles at the base of his skull had exerted an uneven pull from below. The spinal curve itself was due to a patchy muscle loss over his back. Where the muscle on one side of the spine had disappeared, the remaining muscle on the other side had pulled the spine across. Bill had self-diagnosed childhood polio as the cause of this. He became more certain of the diagnosis in his late forties and fifties, when he noticed a prolonged twitching of muscles affecting both his arms and legs. Sometimes there was a weakness associated with the twitching and on one occasion, he couldn't elevate either the thumb or index finger of his right hand. And then, miraculously, the strength had slowly returned and the twitching stopped. The affected muscles had lost volume though and the strength in his thumb and index finger was only eighty per cent restored, rather than fully restored. Following this, getting chilled, for example, by swimming in the sea, there was a rapid onset of hand weakness. It was not unusual for Bill to find himself needing to use both hands to turn the car door key after a sea swim. This didn't stop him bathing however, and he rejoiced in the overall improvement of symptoms, which is unusual in neurological disorders. More commonly, the path is one way, downwards. Being a medical doctor, Bill surmised that he had probably suffered from what is known as a post-polio syndrome. The nerve cells that had been slightly damaged by the virus, or perhaps had been overworked since the initial viral attack, simply gave up the ghost and died off in later life, causing a progression of the initial polio damage. He had not suffered any sensory loss, which fitted in with the polio diagnosis. His mother had told him of a severe febrile illness he had had the night after being vaccinated against polio in the early 1950s. There were polio outbreaks in the country at the time. Bill knew that the vaccine used in those days was a dead form of the virus, given by injection and was unlikely to have caused a problem. He reckoned he had suffered the real thing but had been undiagnosed at the time.

When his thumb and index finger went weak, Bill took himself off to a neurologist. The consultant listened patiently to Bill's theory as to the diagnosis. He examined him and then remained silent for a long time. Bill imagined the great mind considering all sorts of neurological conditions and syndromes, which he had never quite managed to digest himself, from the humourless tomes of neurology textbooks.

Eventually the neurologist broke silence.

"Hmmmm," was all he said.

The silence began again, until being able to stand it no longer, Bill said,

"Shall we see how it goes then?"

"Yes," came the reply. "Come and see me if it gets any worse."

Such was the quality of conversation with all the hallowed brain power of the neurologist behind it. However, it gave the escape cue Bill wanted. He was out of the room as quick as decorum allowed, and vowed he would not be returning, ever.

The reminiscences made Bill smile to himself. He had done all right since then and his crooked spine had caused little trouble. His neck had become painful back in his thirties, but by putting his head through a full range of movement every day and doing a few chin-ups on a bar, Bill had eliminated the pain and was well-pleased with the good function of his back and neck.

The bend in his spine had twisted his ribs a little and this, coupled with an overall reduced muscle bulk on his left side, gave his chest a powerful look on the right and a skinny look on the left. Bill didn't mind. He had the same attitude to his body as he did to his car. If it worked, he was happy.

His bodily mental meanderings took him passed his abdomen, which was flat enough to satisfy him. His tummy was covered with an inch or two of fat which he regarded as his 'reserves'. These reserves were all ready for a rainy day. He kept a check on them though and although six feet tall, Bill weighed only eleven stone and balanced on a line between slim and thin.

Beneath his abdomen, Bill's thoughts descended to his genitals. His pubic hair had greyed a little, as had his head hair but remained curly and thick. His penis was of average size and his inspections of many men in the routine course of his career, had given him a certainty about this. It still pleased him by growing tall and stiff in the early mornings. He referred to it by his own name — William. The skin of both groins was devoid of ordinary sensation, following operations in those areas which had cut the nerves of sensation on both sides, leaving a permanent numbness. The first operation, through the left groin, was done at the age of eleven and was to bring an undescended testicle down into the scrotum. His testicles had had an enormous effect on his life but his testicular ruminations were suddenly stilled, by a distant cry from behind.

"Dr Smith! I am so pleased to have found you!"

He recognised the voice instantly. He turned to see the shapely figure of Mrs Amelia Cordite passing between the tables towards him.

"Bugger," he thought and mentally pushed his testicles to one side.

Amelia was a likeable but formidable lady of the village. She was thc powerhouse behind the town's Christmas decorations, the summer fetes, charity fundraising for numerous needy causes and by no means least, the organiser of the local Women's Institute regular interest talks.

The search for speakers was not an easy one but as soon

as Amelia realised that Bill had worked abroad, he had become a sitting target for her artfully delivered persuasions.

She was wearing a flowered summer frock, which briefly blended with the background roses and ivy as she emerged from the back door of the pub and made her way across to him. The frock shimmered in the breeze, occasionally showing her body shape as the material pressed against her. She was attractive, Bill knew and so did she. Her attractiveness was a great help in wooing reticent speakers for the WI but Bill was not reticent. He had enjoyed giving talks about his past medical adventures. He re-lived them himself as he did so. The problem was that he had exhausted all of his ready-made subjects now. Each and every country he had worked in had been described already, along with the best anecdotes he could muster. The audience were always the same ladies. Repeats were not on the agenda.

Amelia smiled her charming smile at him as she slid onto the table bench opposite. Her face was glowing with health, and her enthusiasm for life twinkled from her eyes, as she caught his gaze.

"Dr Smith," she began, "this is so fortunate. I am at a loss for a speaker for our next WI meeting on Wednesday. They do depend on me so, you know."

"Could that possibly be why you are looking at me?" Bill smiled at her, feeling an intrinsic warmth to her being enhanced by her summer-time attractiveness.

"Well yes, actually, it did cross my mind that you might be able to help us out. You have been such a success before, you know."

"The trouble is, Amelia, I have spoken about the work I've done in every country I have been to. And don't forget, Mrs

Arthbutt passed out last time, when I showed a picture of me doing a caesarean section. I will have to be more thoughtful in future."

"Well, Dr Smith, it was a very bloody image and I fully sympathised with poor Mrs Arthbutt. I do believe she has had two caesarean sections herself and your graphic image was just too much for her."

"You are probably right," answered Bill.

The breeze blew Amelia's brown hair in front of her face. She brushed it aside and sat there displaying a wonderful combination of authority, self-assurance and femininity.

After a few moments of reflection she said,

"Why not talk about something non-medical? After all, you are retired now and your life has opened up a bit. You doctors live a telescopic, cocooned life, miles apart from the rest of us. You are out of that now."

She leaned towards him and he smelt her perfume as she looked him directly in the eye.

"Choose a contentious issue. Give us your take on it. Make us think differently about something. You could be brilliant at that."

It was Bill's turn to ponder. After stroking his still full glass of beer, he returned his gaze to her lively, blue eyes and said,

"Okay then, I will do that Amelia and thanks for the idea. It will do me as much good as anyone. Do you have any ideas about a subject yourself?"

"Good God no!" she snorted. "That's up to you. But you will find something. I have always sensed there is more to you than a wandering quack."

"Wandering quack! That's not a polite way of referring to

my good deeds across the globe, Amelia!"

"Balderdash!" came Amelia's smiling return. "You know as well as I do that you travelled to get away from the boredom of General Practice in England. It was a cheap way of having adventures wherever you wanted and getting paid at the same time. You have said as much!"

She was right and they both knew it. He smiled at her.

"Can I get you a drink?"

"Oh, no thanks. I only popped in on the off-chance and here you were. So, are we agreed then? Next Wednesday evening at 7.30. Don't talk over the hour or they will be asleep."

"Okay, it's a deal. See you then."

She stood up and stood over him. The sunshine caused her hair to sparkle with golden flecks and her body shape was silhouetted through the summer frock.

"I shall look forward to hearing what your new non-medical subject might be. Thank you so much Dr Smith."

With that she was off, passing nimbly between the tables and disappearing through the back door of the pub. Bill realised that Amelia was a femme fatale for him and wondered idly, how Mr Cordite had won her over. She had left him with the challenge of an empty page to write on. Take away medicine and the meat of him was gone. What was he going to talk about?

Quite suddenly, Bill rose briskly from his seat and followed Amelia's track through the bar and into the parking area at the side of the Red Lion. He was just in time to see Amelia pulling smartly away in her red BMW Mini Cooper. With a burst of white exhaust, her car disappeared nimbly into the traffic. He didn't quite know why he had followed her. Had he caught up with her, he had nothing to say. Feeling slightly bewildered by his impulsive pursuit, he ambled back towards his still full glass of Doom Bar beer.

His sudden appearance at the front of the pub had not gone unnoticed by Amelia, who had caught his reflection in her rear-view mirror. She wondered briefly if she had forgotten something, but a sweep of her hand onto the passenger seat confirmed that her handbag was safely there. The traffic was proceeding at an obedient 30mph and she let her mind consider the friendly Doctor a little more. He cut an attractive figure in one way, but appeared unaccountably lonely and consequently a little vulnerable. She guessed he was either divorced or separated from someone. Probably his escapades abroad had done for any home relationship. He was not easy to assess. He was someone who may have reached the end of an active life, but he could just as well be cooking up another outlandish plot. If he was, she wondered, would it be a medical thing or something completely different? Perhaps whatever he came up with for the WI talks would give an insight. She gave a little sigh and pictured for a moment his solitary form as she had found him, contemplating his glass of beer. Then she shook her head, sending her brown hair tumbling and allowed her thoughts to move on.

FATIGUE

This bloody tiredness was annoying him more than worrying him.

He sat down as soon as he got home to his one up, one down maisonette home. His was one quarter of a block — each small home having the same lounge with attached kitchen downstairs and bedroom with adjacent bathroom upstairs. It was ideal for a man living alone, though a big step down from the four-bedroomed bungalow with generous-sized garden that he had left when his divorce came about. That was ten years ago. He cast his mind back across those ten years. The divorce at the start of that time had been a horrible experience, which he would not have inflicted on anyone. He guessed that for some, the experience could be a good and even a painless and sensible option. But the relationship he had with his wife had been good in many respects. She had been a brilliant mother to their children and had loyally supported him, as he laboured through those early hospital jobs. The hours were so long then that he had minimal energy left to help out with the home and children whenever he got home. They had had their children far too early but that was entirely his fault. Obsessed that he might be infertile, he had not used any contraception. Instead of nothing happening, three children had appeared bang, bang, bang. As it turned out, these children became the greatest success of their marriage. The fertility side of things turned out very well. The sexual side of things was not so good. The shared effort of procreation and subsequent labour of love in bringing up the children, had an effect which all parents will recognise. Love-making became tempered by fatigue and reduced by diminished opportunity. A routine developed of Bill's wife merely tolerating his needs and he often found himself in an emotionally lonely place. Whereas his wife had both an accepting and realistic attitude to the change, he was far more bothered. Their marriage had happened at the end of the era when it was still regarded as the gateway to sex. Bill's previous experience was minimal and he certainly had unrealistic expectations when he tied the knot. The accepted restrictions of his married state allowed an unfair resentment of his wife to germinate. Eventually, his curiosity, fuelled by a libido-charged feeling that somehow society had cheated him, led him into forbidden sexual liaisons outside of marriage. He had to wait many years before he had the experience of his sexual partner flushing pink, stiffening and crying out beneath him — but unlike the experiences he had given to his wife, his own journey had been a joyous adventure.

He never called an end to the marriage, partly because he wanted to have the same home address as his children and secondly, because he felt his wife needed him. He was afraid she might fall apart if he left. By the time his wife made the decision for him, the children, who were all adults by then, suggested, rather unkindly he thought, that he should have made the cut himself ten years previously. As for his wife falling apart, not at all. Once she found her feet, she embarked on a brand-new relationship. When that didn't work out, she found another one. He was also dispensed with fairly soon and she had carried on independently, clearly enjoying doing whatever she wanted. The strength of her own personality had emerged. The last time he had met her, he was struck by how well she looked.

Perhaps they had just married too young. He hadn't been mature enough for marriage but maybe she had been. They were both novice lovers and he often wondered if an older, more mature man could have given birth to her own sexual journey, rather than his own sexual blunderings eclipsing it.

He concluded that he had been a poor husband but they could both rejoice over the children they had created. Bill enjoyed reaching brief conclusions after lengthy ponderings.

On the good side, his current relaxed state of mind about women and sex was a result of all those extra experiences. The alternative could have left him an embittered man who disliked women, or worse still, the traditional dirty, old man. He was glad to be neither.

The cost though, had been high. Once, it cost him his job as a GP and he ran the risk of being removed from the General Medical Council's list of Licensed Practitioners. Fortunately, an aggrieved husband had let him off the hook but his job was gone, nonetheless. His wife stuck by him then but when he set up some marriage guidance for them, she didn't engage and soon they were back to square one.

The loss of work was a problem, as a new job required references from the previous one. His partner in General Practice at the time was painfully honest in his appraisal. 'Leaving because of an affair' in a reference, wouldn't pass muster in the conservative world of GPs and so his head had turned towards working abroad. Far fewer questions were asked of the doctors prepared to leave the shores of England. So, unexpectedly, his career took an unplanned turn, which was to both test and thrill him. The various countries where he found work, and the adventures he had, became the stuff of his previous talks to the Women's Institute. He generally glossed over the reason why it had happened. He allowed the impression to float that he had struck out into the world to do good. Amelia had rumbled him though.

Some of his sessions abroad were tough going. It was at the end of his very last foray abroad, to the Democratic Republic of Congo under the auspices of Médecins sans Frontiere, that he came back thin and worn out. He was sixty years old and planned to retire. Bill never knew if it was the build-up of work pressure that made him suddenly do what an errant husband should not do — which was to tell the truth. At least, not if you wanted to stay married. The confessions overwhelmed his wife. Her sense of betrayal soured her memories of their past together and she filed for divorce, on grounds of adultery.

Bill didn't contest the divorce. He thought it was a bad idea but didn't feel he had the right to protest. He didn't blame her either. She must have sensed what he had been up to over many years but she had been able to turn a blind eye. It was quite another thing to have his infidelity spelled out. All of a sudden, his home, his job and his wife were gone.

He experienced the full impact of depression. A feeling of worthlessness enveloped him. His in-laws, whom he had always liked, disappeared, along with some friends. His energy levels dropped and he woke in the mornings bathed in sweat. His early morning mood was always low but gradually improved, enabling him to function as the day wore on. Guilt about not being with a wife who had supported him for so many years was the main thing that gnawed away at him. He never felt suicidal. Instead, he felt a background reassurance that no matter what, at some stage, all this would end.

Eventually he realised that he had to do something about things himself. The main incentive to move forward actually came from his now ex-wife. When she told him that she had found someone else, it came as a relief. She was making her way in the world successfully, now he must do the same.

His first move was to re-enlist as a doctor. He had formally retired on his sixtieth birthday. It took a long time to jump over the hurdles required to regain the medical registration that he had so confidently tossed away a few months previously. His efforts were eventually rewarded with success and after a visit to the General Medical Council office in London to complete the final forms and produce the required evidence of identity, he wandered back onto the London streets, flushed with the knowledge that he could practise as a doctor again.

Bill had no desire to go back into General Practice. The computer-based working lifestyle of modern GPs was not for him. Instead, he joined the Out of Hours Doctors Service and did set sessions covering evenings, nights, weekends and bank holidays when the regular GPs were not available. He didn't overdo the number of sessions he worked but often found himself working late, or through the night.

The job enabled him to get his feet on the ground. His mood slowly improved and with his income boosted, he began exploring hobby interests. First, he sank money and time into microlight flying. These are hang-glider-style aircraft with a pod beneath the wing containing a couple of seats and an engine to power the aircraft skywards. He managed to fulfil his two ambitions of flying across to the Isles of Scilly and later, across the Channel into France.

Having ticked that off his bucket list, he sold the microlight and bought a twenty-eight-foot-long yacht. He had a clear ambition with his new yacht as well. He wanted to do a single-handed sail to Iceland from Falmouth in Cornwall. After three years working on his sailing skills, he managed this feat. Then in the same vein as before, Bill sold the yacht. In between his microlight flying, sailing and working unsociable hours, he also risked another relationship. The person he came close to lived far away from Cornwall, so long car journeys became the norm. However, it wasn't long before an incompatibility between them sent them their separate ways. This time, Bill felt a sadness more than a depression, plus a nagging feeling that perhaps the weak link in relationships might be more to do with him than he had realised before. He wondered what was wrong with him. Friends reassured him that he was a good man, but his confidence in himself dropped.

At seventy, he retired again but a few months later he was surprised to find himself back in the medical harness in response to the Covid-19 viral pandemic. Bill, along with many other recently retired doctors, had been given an emergency registration status, with none of the difficulties he had needed to overcome before. He started doing telephone advisory sessions for a newly created Covid Clinical Assessment Service known as CCAS. The work was easy compared to his previous experiences. He found himself talking to people from all over England who had phoned in with symptoms suggestive of Covid and advising them what course of action to take. However, the return of newly-retired doctors had been unexpectedly enthusiastic, so most sessions were over-staffed. Bill put himself down for night-time sessions when the shifts were more in need of filling. His times were midnight to 4am or 4 am to 8am — which he did alternate nights. When the patient numbers were happily dwindling, he stopped the sessions and placed himself on a reserve list, in case the need recurred.

Now he was feeling tired. It was more than tired, it was a through the body weakness, coupled with a mild aching all over and loss of drive to accomplish just about anything. Strangely, he felt confident that he wasn't ill — not with an illness anyone could put a label on anyway. Bill knew that doctors were notorious for not reporting symptoms until an average policeman could make the diagnosis but he resolutely stayed away from the Doctors' surgery. He considered how he would have thought about his symptoms had he been treating or advising himself, which of course he was.

Excluding fatigue caused by an illness or disease which was an obvious cause, such as cancer, chronic fatigue comes in different forms. The acute and healthy form was the normal feeling of tiredness that comes after running a mile flat-out. That required several minutes to get over, and in health, left the person feeling stronger. A more prolonged mental or physical effort may require a weekend or a week's holiday to recover from. Bill had done a couple of marathons in his younger days. His times were slow at four hours twenty-five minutes for the first one and four hours twenty minutes for the second one (which was twenty years after the first). The thing was, slow as they were, Bill had put all he had to give into the effort. After each marathon, it took six weeks before he felt any desire to go running again.

Then, there is the more subtle form of prolonged fatigue. The various names given to it are chronic fatigue syndrome, post-viral syndrome, myalgic encephalomyelitis, better known simply as ME, serotonin deficiency syndrome, or more recently, burnout. In days gone by, a 'nervous breakdown' was the description given to the point at which someone ran out of steam and became unable to function.

Bill didn't know if these conditions were all caused by the same underlying process but he thought it likely. The linking factor was that the body's stock of mental energy, which has a chemical form, was all used up. Viral damage could be particularly vicious in reducing normal production of these vital chemicals within the brain. Glandular fever in youngsters was well known to leave a trail of disabling fatigue behind it and so could prolonged physical or mental stress. Some people would have more natural resilience and reserve than others, in just the same way that some people are taller than others. On top of this came the effects of different personality traits, varying from the endless striver and achiever, to the downright lazy. Everyone is unique.

If he added up his own activity and stress levels over the past ten years, it was quite impressive. Bill totted up the causative factors as loss of job, alongside his loss of wife and home. Then came the effort of setting up a new home alone and regaining work with late or night-time working hours. In microlighting and sailing he had given himself ambitious targets to hit and had worked hard enough to achieve them. He had tried another relationship, which had also failed, and now, here he was again, at the end of doing another series of night-time working sessions.

The simple fact was that he was burning up a little more

mental and physical energy than his body had to give. There was also the extra half hour being up at night, when he should have gone to bed. The runs which he loved to do, when perhaps he should have been chatting with family, or simply enjoying a pint of beer, or watching a film. It was a tendency he had readily recognised in others but was slow to accept in himself. Bill knew the problem often took hold of someone with a driving and strong personality, who initially sailed successfully along through life at a high pace, because they were young and had plenty of reserve. When the reserve was all used up, which might take many years, there was a bewilderment that a couple of early nights hadn't restored them to normal. Often there was also anger and frustration at doctors who failed to come up with a medical reason. Usually, the best treatment came down to gentle activities which were gradually increased. But it wasn't easy for an athlete to reduce his daily exercise to a fifty metre walk a day and then to patiently build things up, by slowly adding in short periods of jogging as well. The very good news was that, eventually, most people got better. Cognitive Behavioural Therapy, or CBT, seemed to be the best way of leading people out of the valley.

His ultimate summing up was so simple it made him smile. He had been over doing it and needed to chill out. He wasn't all the way down the track of chronic fatigue but he was part way down and needed to change his lifestyle. His love of running had faded, his interest in sex had dwindled, his very enjoyment of life was dimmed. This was another one of Bill's self-diagnoses on the same lines that his diagnosis of childhood polio had been. It was enough to stop him worrying, just as his polio diagnosis had reassured him. It also gave him a simple plan to deal with it. It was just a question of getting the balance of life right.

Bill was happy with the results of his ruminations. He didn't think he was significantly depressed because of the immediate lift he felt when talking to the likes of Amelia. He needed to chill out all right and it wasn't a matter of just a few early nights. It had taken him ten years to get to feel so damned weak and feeble, so he was talking about weeks and months of relative rest, to restore those old feelings of energy.

Bill prepared to take his easier lifestyle very seriously. He needed to get better, to feel strong again. He had things to do.

It never occurred to him that he was now seventy years old and there might be another factor at work.

THE FIRST WOMEN'S INSTITUTE TALK

The day of the first non-medical talk he had ever given arrived.

About 9am on the Wednesday morning, the telephone had rung. It was Amelia.

"Are you still okay for this evening, Doctor?"

"Hello Amelia. Yes, everything's ready. I imagine you will give some kind of introduction?"

"Yes indeed, Dr Smith. I have told several ladies already that you are giving the talk and they are really pleased. I think we can expect a good turn out."

By a good turnout, Bill knew that Amelia was talking about twenty people. That was a lovely number as far as he was concerned. It was cosy, intimate and gave plenty of opportunity for questions. He was looking forward to it.

"What did you decide to talk about then?"

"Northern Ireland."

"Good God doctor! What in heavens name for? Aren't the Troubles there, ancient history anyway?"

"Not exactly ancient history, no," he replied. "There is plenty of room for improvement, as you will see."

He felt a little uneasy at the strength of her reaction. Amelia was not someone to let her feelings go unnoticed.

"But, but, what does it have to do with us? And anyway, isn't it all terribly complicated for ordinary people to understand?"

"Everything has something to do with us Amelia, from people drowning in the Mediterranean Sea, to planting bombs in Northern Ireland. They are ordinary people over there by the way, just like you and me, and solutions to problems don't have to be complicated."

He was beginning to feel assertive. "The question for us is what, if anything, do we want to do about it?"

"Well, it's certainly a first for the Women's Institute here Doctor. Northern Ireland. Heavens above! Anyway, I shall be behind you all the way. And let's face it, without you and Northern Ireland suddenly rising up out of the blue, we wouldn't have anything at all. It is a surprise though, bless you."

She was mellowing.

"See you later then." He put the phone down, feeling slightly rattled.

He left his home an hour before the talk was due to start and ambled along the tidy pavements towards the Red Lion pub. It was his habit to have a beer before public speaking, though wine or champagne at weddings also relaxed him nicely. The pub was situated half-way to the Women's Institute hall and he had, over the years, developed an easy routine for these talks. Evening sunshine warmed him as a light breeze wafted past him. He had learned to enjoy the gentle sensations of England, after the more strident stimulations of faraway lands. He passed the pub car park, which was partly hidden by an unkempt escallonia hedge. The scent of blossom filled his nostrils as he walked onwards to the pub entrance. Pushing open the bar door, he entered the lounge bar and even though the summer was at its height, a wood fire glowed and smoked in the large fire grate to his right, as he passed towards the bar. Most of the clientele were obediently spaced, following the Covid-19 social distancing directives, although a group of noisy, young men seated around the fire were stretching the regulations by thoughtless proximity to each other. They were laughing in the unseemly way that young men do, when drunk. Bill didn't mind that at all. He had been dangerously drunk once and had been so unaware of his actions that anything could have happened. He was a medical student at the time. He had been saved by his friends, who had laid him face down, having heaved him, unconscious onto a bed. His last clear memory had been drinking a tumbler full of brandy, as a dare, early on at his flatmate's twenty-first birthday party. He woke up the next morning with his face covered in his own sticky vomit. In retrospect, he realised that the vomiting had probably got some of the alcohol out of his stomach, but it was the thoughtful positioning of him on the bed by his friends that had stopped him from drowning in it. Since then, Bill had avoided significant drunkenness. He enjoyed his drinks though. Genetics had favoured him by installing the hard wiring to give him maximum pleasure from the first drink, with ever diminishing desire for subsequent chasers. All the people Bill had met who were struggling with alcohol had been hard-wired the other way around.

The barman was the landlord of the pub and knew Bill well.

"The usual Bill?" he enquired.

"Thank you, Martin, yes please," he replied, glancing at Martin — who had evolved over the years from acquaintance to friend. "What's the best with you then?"

"I'm just enjoying the summer, old boy. At least we are not completely shut down now by this bloody virus. There was enough in our piggy bank to keep us going, thank heavens." Martin had a contented look about him. His roundish face was relaxed, though as Bill glanced at his substantial girth, he mentally changed his assessment of Martin from content to over content.

"I hear you are giving the WI talk tonight," Martin continued. "Is this your limber up for it?"

"It is indeed," Bill replied, savouring a generous mouthful of his favourite Doom Bar beer. "This will get me going. Makes all the difference you know."

"Well, I hope you get them going too," replied Martin. He gave a sigh that suddenly didn't sound contented at all.

"Sweet fanny adam happens here, Bill. I need something to get me going as well. I feel a bit short of action. I'm in a bloody rut!"

"Get on with you." Bill felt the need to encourage his friend. "We all depend on you to get oil between the cogs. Life wouldn't be the same without you."

"Too much bloody oil sometimes," said Martin, nodding towards the group of lads as their laughter once again reverberated around the room. "Definitely too much bloody oil."

Bill quietly finished his drink as Martin left to serve the next customers. He slipped into the gents, as he knew his glass of beer would result in a rapid filling of his bladder. Then, feeling fully prepared, he made his way past the noisy youths, walked purposefully down the road and entered the Woman's Institute hall.

The hall was an inauspicious but neat building, with granite walls supporting a dark grey, slated roof. The wooden door and window frames to either side of it were painted green and a single granite step led up from the pavement to the entrance.

Amelia was greeting all comers just inside. Previously, she had greeted Bill for his talks with an enthusiastic pumping handshake. This evening, it was a whack from her elbow on his, with no diminution of enthusiasm at all.

"So glad to see you Doctor," she beamed confidently at him. "You are the most important person in the room."

"Thanks Amelia," he said, "I'll try not to disappoint then."

"No chance of that Doctor, now come along with me. We are listening to you first, so you can beetle off afterwards, as you won't want to be listening to our business matters, will you?"

"Indeed no," he replied, feeling genuinely grateful to be getting on with things.

So it was only ten minutes after his arrival that he found himself standing to face his audience, who hushed politely in expectation, as soon as he stood to his feet. Glancing around, he was pleased to see some young faces amongst the regular stalwarts. They were obediently separated from each other, as the Covid regulations required. A few of them wore face coverings but most did not. He also noticed a single male face, at the back. His gaze lingered briefly on the man. He looked both alert and relaxed at the same time. His close-cropped, thick, brown hair and fresh facial features reminded him of someone but he couldn't place the connection.

He cleared his throat and began, speaking loudly and clearly, quickly relaxing into the task as the sound of his voice filled the room.

"Ladies and gentleman," he said, giving a tiny nod to the single male listener, "we are going to consider a small aspect of a big problem, here in the UK. You will all have heard a lot about it, over many years. I am talking this evening about Northern Ireland."

It was immediately evident that Amelia had not informed everybody about the subject. Mutters of 'Northern Ireland!' and 'Good heavens above!' reached his ears through the murmurings of sound, from whispered comments and a restless fidgeting which briefly spread through the room.

"It seems a bit rich for me to talk about Northern Ireland," he went on, "after all, I have never been there. But, like most English people, I have heard of the Troubles and felt a mixture of horror and puzzlement at the violence going on. It is greatly improved now, compared to their worst times, but Belfast is still divided by a wall, ironically called the Peace Wall, and outbreaks of the old violent ways are cropping up again.

"I have met several Irish people over the years and have found them likeable without exception. I have also admired the Irish rugby team, with their unpredictable ability to disrupt the power of the best of English rugby teams, against all odds.

"As a rule, I didn't talk about the Troubles with the Irish people I have met but on one occasion, I did. I was chatting to a young person involved with youth work in Belfast and put to her the question — "Wouldn't it help if all the children went to thc same schools, instead of religiously segregated schools?"

Her answer was an unambiguous, "Yes." She also pointed out that this was already happening on a small scale.

Back in the 1980s, I listened to two men of the church

being interviewed on the radio. They were asked for their ideas on improving relations within the community. One was a Catholic Priest, the other a Protestant Minister. They were quietly spoken, with nothing strident or unsettling in their manner. The Christian message of love and forgiveness was shared by both of them, together with ideas of practical inter-community support. Then they were asked if it would be better if the children from Catholic and Protestant communities shared the same schools, so they could get to know each other. In their gentle and soothing ways, they both explained why they preferred their own special messages of spiritual guidance not to be diluted by the influence of the other.

What these gentle voices were actually saying was

'LET THE BATTLE CONTINUE!'"

Bill raised his voice to emphasise the point. The room was absolutely silent.

He paused for effect, before continuing,

"Why did they say this? Is it a fear of losing their own influence?

"Let me tell you this, ladies and gentleman, all of our thoughts, words and deeds originate from either a place of fear, or a place of love.

"These men were coming from a place of fear.

"To quote another who was describing life in Belfast at the worst time of their Troubles: 'Hatred is imbibed with their mother's milk.' One thing is for sure, hatred is a learned thing. When a baby is born into a Catholic family, it doesn't have any more ideas about Catholicism than a baby born down the road into a Protestant family has of Protestantism. They learn what their community teaches them and especially what their parents tell them. If their parents, in turn, have been subjected to abuse, fear and attack from their neighbours, then it is only natural to pass their reactions down the line and burden the new innocents with the same."

Bill paused and checked to see if he still had his audience with him. They were definitely paying attention. He felt more confident.

"Imagine this," he said. "A teenage boy playing rugby in his school team, takes a pass from his mate and slices through the opposition to score the winning try. Those two youngsters will have forged a bond that is more knowing and more significant than any take on religion. They learn about each other and know each other's strengths and weaknesses at a human level. What religion their mum and dad follow drops into perspective, as the youngsters have the experience of realising that they are all the same, whichever Church they were born into. It ceases to be them and us. Them and us become the same. School life offers so much more than rugby. Shared schooling provides a chance to produce a generation that doesn't want to suffer the pain of one section fearing and fighting another section. They are far more likely to want to repair any injustices they come across in society, simply because they know and understand that they are all the same.

"That's not rocket science, is it?"

Bill checked his audience with a scanning glance — it seemed okay, they were still with him.

"I talked about how we all come from a position of love or fear. So what's the fearful response then? Well, it will be something like this: 'We can't trust these people. We need to be defended against them. If they attack us, we will hit back so hard that they will regret it forever'.

"Does that sound familiar? Have you ever heard that sort

of rhetoric coming out of the Israeli-Palestinian conflict?

"How about looking at it from a position of love: We want the best for our children. Why subject them to the same tragedies we faced? If we allow them to meet in schools — which might teach about religion but don't push any particular version of it — we can give them a chance to make their own decisions. Does it really matter anyway? So long as our young people think about it and make their own minds up, surely that's okay. And anyway, do we really think, deep down, that God will accept one group and reject another, simply because of the style of church they do or don't attend?

"I am asking everyone of you, to think about this and decide for yourself. Would this be a worthwhile change? Or do you agree with the two churchmen I heard on the radio, all those years ago? It would be a small change, but even small changes need strong leadership to implement. I am asking you as individuals to turn your brains on and decide how you feel. And remember this: not to make a decision, is in fact a decision. It means that you accept the status quo and are going to do nothing to change it. No decision is an important decision.

"So long as you have switched on your brain and made your personal decision, that is all I am asking of you.

"Perhaps the best way of putting any issue to yourself is not to ask, is this right or is it wrong? Ask rather, does this work for us? If not, can we make it work better?

"If something is working, leave well alone. If not, look for the change that will make it work.

"The Irish lady who told me that this change is already taking place on a small scale, had no doubts about the benefits. It must be possible to accelerate it. Northern Ireland has an opportunity to turn its nightmare of fear and violence into such an example of love in action, that the rest of the world will have a class act to follow.

"So I say,

'Come on Ireland!

Come on Ireland!

Come on Ireland'!"

Bill shouted the last few words and banged his fist down on the table in front of him, making a small, glass jar of flowers jump up and land with a clatter, scattering droplets of water.

The room remained absolutely silent.

TROUBLE AT THE RED LION

Amelia had eventually started off a round of clapping and had given a polite thank you speech. She had struggled a bit, with words such as surprising, different and challenging coming to her, as she clearly didn't quite know how to frame her response.

Bill didn't care, although he wondered briefly if that would be his last ever invite from Amelia to talk to the WI. He noticed as he edged out of the room that the buzz of conversation was finding an increasing volume. He noticed the single male member of the audience whisper something briefly in Amelia's ear, before he left the room, ahead of Bill.

"Maybe I have got them thinking." Bill murmured to himself. He felt pleased to have given the talk, irrespective of their reaction. The subject had been a bee in his bonnet for years.

The summer evening had slid into early darkness as he made his way home and feeling a little subdued as the intensity of his talk began to fade, it seemed a well-deserved diversion to pop into the Red Lion for a final pint of bitter on his way home. He strode briskly towards the Red Lion, taking in deep breaths as he went and allowing a tension within him to subside. He loved the soft darkness of English summer evenings and this particular evening was providing a feeling of warmth and security, feelings which an analyst would have noted were in short supply in his mindset. He brushed passed the escallonia hedgerow once again, savouring the scent which struck him even more forcibly than before and pushed open the age-old oaken door of the pub and entered.

He made his way to the far end of the bar, where his habit was to rest on a bar stool and chat to Martin, as and when he was free. Behind him was a small passageway leading to the toilets. He found his way to his favourite spot in the far corner of the room but just as he was reaching out for the bar stool, he was pushed roughly to one side. A startled glance showed him that one of the drunken group he had seen previously, had emerged from the toilets and had made a direct line to the bar, scarcely noticing Bill was there. Bill wasn't too fragile a personality to be over bothered by the incident but watched with increasing alarm, as the drunken youth leaned across the top of the bar shouting loudly,

"Where's those beers, fatty?"

He was looking at Martin, who came towards him looking uneasy.

"You and your friends have had more than enough. If you don't clear off, as I said, I will call the police." Martin looked uneasy but spoke loud and clear.

"Come here you fucker!" With surprising speed, the large, young man leaned across the bar and yanked Martin by his shirt top right over the bar, so their noses were just inches apart. Martin's neck was being compressed by a powerful grip around his collar and his face was rapidly turning purple. Bill realised that he was trying to speak but couldn't. His assailant was well-covered in fat but powerful as well. A lot of weight. Too bad.

Several times in the past, Bill had reacted on pure instinct. He had twice found himself engaged in fights with violent, agitated patients, when more considered responses had deserted him.

This was another such occasion. He slid a dinner fork from its serviette wrapper and stepped up to Martin's attacker. The white T-shirt he was wearing had pulled upwards from his waist, exposing a four-inch expanse of skin. Bill plunged the fork into his side.

Whilst pros and cons of the decision to stab the man never reached Bill's consciousness, other things did. His grip on the fork was low down the handle and his thumb rested just an inch below the tip of the prongs. He wanted to inflict pain, not serious injury, and this grip would prevent penetration beyond an inch. Bill's surgical experience was such that he knew this man would be covered in more than an inch of fat. As he pressed the fork home, the skin stretched far inwards under the pressure, until a tiny pop indicated that it had been breached. The effect was dramatic. With a huge intake of breath, the man released his grip from Martin's neck and stared disbelievingly at Bill.

"What the fuck have you done?" he seethed.

He looked down at his side where a drop of blood had emerged from the punctured skin and begun to roll down.

"You fucking asshole! You are completely fucked now!"

Bill's mind was now working well. He didn't like the situation at all though. He had leaned close to the man as he stabbed him with the fork and caught a glimpse of a knife handle, resting in a sheath sewn to the inside of his pocket. In his forties, Bill had attended Tae Kwando lessons for five years. He was never a great student of the art but had learned a few tricks, that he thought might turn out useful if he was ever in a tight spot. One of the Tae Kwando games that Bill had always enjoyed was when the students did mock attacks on each other, using a plastic knife. Bill had invariably found himself harmlessly stabbed in these encounters and his subsequent mind-set was always to look for escape if confronted. But there was no escape here. Behind him was the toilet door with a lethal dead-end beyond it. Around the side of this big, angry man there was a bit of a squeeze to get by in normal circumstances. He was going to have to fight. How to get this man down? He was huge compared to Bill. It had to be a disabling pain to stop him; far more than the pain caused by the fork. His eyes, perhaps, or testicles? Bill braced. He didn't feel good but by God if he was going down, he would go down fighting.

He saw the hand drop onto the knife handle and flick off a restraining loop. Bill kicked back his stool to give himself space. There was no way out now.

"I wouldn't do that if I were you."

The voice came quietly from behind Bill's shoulder. Quiet though it was, there was an arresting quality to it which turned the heads of both Bill and the seething young man.

Standing to one side of Bill, was the fresh-faced man he had spotted at the back of the Women's Institute hall. The face was calm, focussed and in an inexplicable way, unnerving. Perhaps it was the total absence of fear, or maybe the unspoken confidence it exuded.

"You are drunk," he went on, "you won't be able to defend yourself. If you pull that knife, I can assure you that within a few seconds you will be feeling a lot more pain than the pin prick he just gave you," he said, nodding briefly towards Bill.

There was silence. It seemed as though the young man was beginning to take in warning signs. He was slowly registering, that suddenly, another strangely calm and confident opposition had appeared. The silence persisted, though Bill became aware of Martin's hoarse breathing in the background.

The stranger looked across at the group the man was with. There were four of them, all gawping at their friend.

"Take him home. He is about to get himself hurt. Come on!" The last was a military style command which snapped across the room like a whip.

Bill was now confident that his salvation must have come from some form of military man. He was truly impressed and a melting feeling of relief washed over him. His opponent was no more. He was deflating in front of their eyes. His friends shambled over, put their arms though his and led him slowly out. As they cleared the door, a spontaneous round of applause rippled through the room from the bewildered customers. Bill became the most enthusiastic applauder of them all.

The stranger gave a brief smile, before following the lads out through the door. He was back in a few seconds, scribbling something on the back of his hand.

"Give me your phone please," he asked Martin. "They are driving away, pissed as newts, so maybe we can get the local bobbies to round off their evening. I've got the car number."

Once the phone call had been completed, he turned to Bill and Martin and said,

"Gents, I will catch up with you later. There's a lady who will probably be ready for me at the WI hall by now. I had taken the liberty of parking in the Red Lion car park and had just popped in for a pee."

Looking straight at Bill he said,

"Take care now, I am sure we will meet again."

He strode across the room. As he reached the door, Bill shouted after him,

"What's your name?"

"Cordite," he replied, "Alan Cordite." Then he was gone.

A thud on the bar beside Bill announced the arrival of a pint of beer from Martin, which was exactly what he was feeling in need of.

"I won't forget that Bill, ever." Martin's voice was a bit hoarse and his neck had been reddened by the compression.

"Here I was, telling you that nothing ever happened here. Ha!"

"Well, don't say it again, for God's sake!" replied Bill. "We were lucky though, both of us."

"Who was that guy? Had you ever seen him before?"

"Yes, but only once," said Bill, taking a sip of his beer. He was surprised to notice as he did that his hand was trembling. "He was at the Women's Institute when I gave the talk. His name, Cordite, is the same as the woman who arranges things there. He must be her husband."

"Bloody lucky he needed a pee when he did," declared Martin. "Otherwise, we'd still be sweeping you up."

"Yes, impressive, wasn't he? He stopped everything from going completely tits up by just using his tongue."

"No," said Martin, "it was a bloody sight more than just his tongue. You could smell the muscle on him and that cold look he had would put the fear of God into anyone. Who would want to test him out?"

"Well Martin," Bill raised his glass, "some of us have it

and some of us don't. So let us salute those who do!" He took a hearty gulp before adding, "And he certainly does!"

The second pint of beer had dropped comfortably into Bill's stomach before he set off for home. The streets were quiet and the summer darkness felt soft in the residual evening warmth. Some of the larger stones on garden walls were palpably radiating heat. Bill felt soothed by the feeling of it all but was still unsettled by the suddenness of his foray into a danger zone and the near miraculous escape.

He let himself in to his tiny home and ignoring the busy, red flashing from his telephone answering machine, he went upstairs, taking the steps two at a time and ran himself a deep bath. He moderated the temperature to fit the warm evening ambience, lowered himself gently into it and sighed gently at the pleasure of it all.

"That was not a good start to me taking life a bit easier," he thought briefly. His eyelids began to fall and he soon surrendered himself to the embrace of the water.

Waking up was still not Bill's favourite time of day. Normally, he appointed that time of day for either a morning run or an exercise routine which lasted about thirty minutes. Not today though. He had decided to give himself lay-ins from now on and to go running or to work out only when the desire to do so felt strong. Previously, his waning energy had required him to make an ever-increasing effort to maintain his exercise routine. Eventually he had capitulated. Bill hoped his energy levels would return before too long. For now though, he accepted where he was in life.

His restful lie-in had only lasted five minutes when the ringing of the downstairs phone roused him again. He got to it just before the answerphone cut in, clad in his silk dressing gown patterned with oriental figures.

"Hello."

"Dr Smith! What a relief to hear you! I have been quite beside myself. You haven't answered any of my messages and Alan told me about the awful incident in the pub. It sounds just, well, awful. How are you anyway? There is such a lot I want to talk to you about. Oh, by the way, your talk was a great success — which is jolly surprising considering the subject. I couldn't get them to stop going on about it. It took forever to get on to the business part of the meeting. And why did you slip away so quickly? There were loads of questions. You will have to come back soon, you know. Anyway, we were late home and then Alan told me about your own horrible experience. Neither of us would have known anything about it if he hadn't just popped into the pub to use the loo. He was supposed to be fetching the car to come and pick me up. Oh, you poor, brave man. Are you okay? Tell me how you are."

"I'm all the better for hearing you, Amelia." Bill meant it. Her enthusiasm, as always, was very unpredictable in direction but she was again, giving him a welcome mental lift.

"You are a sweet creature," she cooed back. "Look, Alan is off on duty again this afternoon. We don't know where he is going or how long for. It's just hopeless really but, if he can accept it, then I had better jolly well accept it as well. He said, why don't you come around this morning for coffee, so you can see both of us before he goes. Now Doctor, are you free?"

"That would be lovely. I would like to thank Alan as well. He got me out of a tight spot yesterday."

"Oh, he's always doing that sort of thing. I think he read too many Boys Own comics when he was a boy. Maybe you'll be able to get him to mature a bit — who knows!" She laughed.

Bill thought she was maybe underestimating her husband. Anyway, it would be good to talk to both of them, for different reasons.

"What time shall I come?"

"We have coffee at eleven."

The drive to the Cordite's home took him through the town centre, passed the bank, a new supermarket, a large garden centre and onwards between green fields and wooded areas beyond. He sped under huge electric pylons and glanced sideways at their solid march across the countryside, heading somewhere down west. A left turning removed him from the busyness of the main route out of town and into a smaller country road. It was full of blind bends, bordered by high Cornish hedges and, as he slowed to negotiate them, his eyes glimpsed leaf-laden hedgerows bedecked with pin pricks of yellow honeysuckle. A short driveway on the right, signed with the house name of Clifton House, took him to a gravel driveway. He scrunched his way slowly along it to park at one side of a large front door. On the other side of the door, was parked an old silver-coloured Seat Toledo. The boot was open and various kit bags were visible inside. Bill surmised that this was Alan's vehicle in preparation for departure. He checked his watch, 10.58hrs. Excellent. He emerged from his red-coloured Micra and stretched, before walking up to the substantial-looking, old house and ringing the doorbell.

The sound of rapid footsteps heralded a dramatic opening of the front door and there was Amelia, beaming at him with arms outstretched.

"Doctor Smith. Hello!" she exclaimed. "Let me give you

a hug!"

Social distancing thrown to the winds, he felt her arms envelope him and the soft pressure of her body uninhibitedly pressed against his. The hug was a long one and as she released him to candidly appraise him at arm's length, he could only return her gaze with a feeling of genuine pleasure. Social distancing had certainly been swept aside.

"Come in now, Doctor. Coffee is almost ready. I will call Alan down, as he said he wanted a word with you anyway."

They passed through the solid oak front door, into a tiled hallway.

"You haven't got a coat or anything have you?" she checked with him. "If you did you could dump them here." She waved towards a line of wall hooks already laden with a variety of coats, anoraks and wet weather gear. Beneath was a collection of shoes and green wellington boots. He was wearing only a T-shirt and blue chinos; the weather still remaining deliciously warm. Beyond the hooks was a doorway on the right. Straight ahead, a second doorway clearly led into her kitchen. Bill could see a large back garden through the kitchen window, which was situated above the sink unit. On the left, at the end, the hallway led into a darker looking corridor. Midway along, on the left, a staircase led upwards. Amelia paused at the lower end of it and shouted up,

"Alan, Doctor Smith is here!"

Turning back to Bill she said,

"Come this way Doctor," and she guided him through the doorway on the right, into an airy and spacious lounge.

"Do have a seat."

"Thanks," replied Bill and added "please call me Bill, Amelia. It's my name after all and my doctor days end anytime now." He went on to explain how he was putting himself on the reserve list of doctors to help with the Covid-19 virus pandemic, thus hopefully signalling the end of a forty-five year-long medical career.

"Oh," said Amelia," I thought you had retired already. Anyway, Bill it is from now on then," she declared. "Perhaps when Alan leaves, we should celebrate this momentous change in your life with a glass of champagne. Alan for sure won't be touching any, as he has a decent drive to do shortly. Do you like champagne Doctor, oh, sorry! Bill?"

"I do," said Bill smiling.

Alan arrived shortly after, wearing well-used deck shoes and blue denim jeans and shirt. His sleeves were rolled halfway up his forearms, revealing smooth and well-defined musculature. His arms were those of a rock climber, strong enough to support his weight and trust his life to the grip of his fingers. Sandy-coloured hairs covered his forearms, which gave a flash of ginger in the sunlight. Bill was briefly transfixed by the appearance. The hairs were short, neat, almost downy. Their softness contrasted greatly with the masculinity he possessed.

He was well groomed, clean shaven, his neat, close-cropped and thick, brown hair was tidy about him. His face was lined, which Bill had not noticed before. He guessed him to be about fifty years of age. The lines gave him an impression of ruggedness which was accentuated by a faint, white scar running straight down the side of his left cheek. His eyes were light blue and Bill still found his direct gaze disconcerting. The overall effect was of extreme physical well-being. He was the sort of man Bill had always wanted to be.

He rose to greet him.

"Hello again," he said. "I'm Bill Smith. I've just asked Amelia to drop the Dr bit, as I am retiring any day now anyway."

"Good morning, Bill," Alan replied with a friendly smile, showing unblemished teeth. "Have you got over the fracas of last night?"

"Yes, but it did affect me. I was literally shaking afterwards."

Amelia entered at that moment and placed a large tray laden with milk jugs, two full coffee cafetieres and a plate laden with expensive-looking luxury biscuits. The phone rang just as the tray touched the table.

"Oh, for fuck's sake!" Amelia's swearing made Bill smile. "I had better answer it," she went on, "I'm sorry Doc, or rather Bill, if it's the call from America about some cut glass I am waiting for, I shall have to deal with it and I may be a while. He's phoning me at some God forsaken hour over there, so I can't leave it. Alan will sort you out anyway."

She strode out to answer the phone and shortly afterwards, her voice echoed from the next room. "It is my call boys, talk amongst yourselves!"

Alan did indeed sort things out and Bill was soon relaxing with a bone china mug filled with white coffee in his hand and a couple of chocolate biscuits on the plate beside him.

"Tell me Bill," Alan asked quietly "have you had any thoughts about last night, after time to reflect?"

"You bet!" replied Bill. "I acted on impulse and got myself into deep water. If you hadn't turned up when you did, I was, as they say, up shit creek."

"Have you ever got into that sort of trouble before, by being impulsive?"

"Yes," said Bill, "twice actually. The first time it was a lady who had hypomania. She was a patient, which makes it even worse. Hypomania just means she was mentally overactive, sort of over the top, really out of control. She had tried to buy three cars that day. I was called to help by her friend, who was being terrified by her. I found her in the friend's house and told her I would take her to the local hospital and give her something to help. The trouble is that anybody in that state is completely unaware that they need help. She told me to fuck off but when she tried to walk past me, I stood right in front of her and barred the way. She gave me a wallop on my shoulder with her arm held straight. I just grabbed the arm, twisted the wrist and forced her to the ground. Before either of us realised what was happening, I found myself sitting on her backside, holding her arm in a half nelson. You won't find that method of management in the medical text books!"

"Impressive," returned Alan, "how did you get yourself out of that little mess?"

"I got the friend to bring my bag over and injected her with enough diazepam to get her asleep. The friend also called the ambulance. I had them take her up to the local cottage hospital and was sat beside her when she woke up. I was half hoping the injection would have at least dulled her memory. No such luck. The second she saw me she hissed, "I will get you for this Doctor!"

"So she sued you then?"

"She wanted to. But I had, just the week before, done a small operation on her elderly mother — to remove a stitch from an old hernia repair which had caused an abscess. Her mother thought I was the best thing since sliced bread and wouldn't let her daughter follow up. Lucky, eh?"

"You were lucky, yes," said Alan, nodding with a slightly amused look on his face. "And the second time?"

"I was half way through a routine surgery when an angry patient barged in as I was talking to someone else. He was shouting at me for cutting down on his diazepam and the way he was behaving, he probably had a point! The patient I had been seeing literally sprinted out of the room. I remember being amused by that because he had hobbled in complaining of back ache. The angry patient then marched passed me and I followed right behind. He turned suddenly and I anticipated a punch coming and shot my arm up to deflect it. The only thing I deflected was his nose as he was turning to face me. His head was jerked backwards, which definitely didn't improve his temper. He yelled, "Oh, you want a fight do you!" He flung a punch which caught my right forehead. It wasn't much but I hit him back anyway. We sparred for a couple of minutes. I can remember how unreal it all felt. Eventually, he charged me into the wall and we were both panting like old men. I said, 'Shall we just sit down now and talk this over?' Before he could answer, the door shot open again and the police charged in and hoiked him outside."

Alan's amusement was clearly increasing. "How did that wonder of medical management turn out?"

"After a while, I went outside and found him in tears, talking to the policemen. He was scared stiff about fighting with a doctor, in case he got sent to prison. Amazingly, he wanted to stay on my list. I expect his previous doctors had all found good reasons to throw him off their own lists. I am not too fazed by mild fisticuffs like that. We both had a couple of small bruises, nothing really. I sat down beside him and had a little chat. I ended up saying he could stay on my list, thanked the policemen for their help and told them they could go. The two of us got on fine after that."

"Interesting," said Alan, with a more thoughtful look on his face. "In my line, we take getting out of trouble as seriously as we do getting into it. The second bit is often the tricky part but your technique of relying on luck worked well again for you last night."

"So what line are you in Alan?" This was the opening Bill had been hoping for.

"Special forces, various types," he replied simply, "I don't do much myself these days, it's mainly training work for me now. I've done my share of the spadework."

"Did you come through unscathed?"

"In the important sense I think and hope so, yes. By that I mean I feel mentally okay. Some of my mates are struggling mentally. There is stress whenever human beings behave violently to each other. That's why you were shaking last night."

"How about physically?"

"I was injured twice. Once I was shot in the thigh and groin. The top bullet wrote off a testicle the other two left holes in my thigh but missed the bone and big blood vessels. I didn't realise I had been hit 'til the fighting stopped. No long-term harm done though. Then there was a knife slash which caught my cheek but I was able to deal with him okay."

Bill felt subdued. His stories sounded absurd when delivered to a warrior like Alan.

Alan carried on. "I did want to talk to you about last night. I see now that you can be impulsive and therefore more likely to get into trouble. You weren't actually in trouble last night.

You just thought you were. The problem for you was that you had stopped thinking."

He paused, as they both savoured their coffee and Bill munched his biscuits before Alan continued,

"As soon as you kicked that stool away, I knew you would need a hand. That stool was a handy tool. You could have held it up to keep him away from you, shoved it into his face, hurt him a bit. You didn't even notice the fire extinguisher behind you. That would have been an excellent ploy, a blast of foam giving you time to get passed him. If all that failed, the toilet door behind you was waiting to be used as a barrier while you raised seven bells, shouting for help behind it. Noise frightens bullies who know they are in the wrong, so shout and shout again. It's harder for on-lookers to resist helping anybody that's shouting for help." Alan paused as he finished his coffee.

"The biggest mistake was how you attacked him. You had surprise on your side. He was drunk and focussed on the barman. So why attack him from a position where he can turn and box you in? There is some danger from a big, drunk man like that. If he got his hands on you, you were going down. That miserable bugger had a knife as well. So why not squeeze passed him first, before you attack and get into a safe position? Then ram the fork in as hard as you can. You can guarantee he would have let go of the barman. Meanwhile, you have legged it out the door. That would have been a decent plan of attack. Your exit strategy is properly worked out. You have done your job and don't end up a dead hero. See what I mean?"

He went on,

"You did a couple of things right, mind. A dinner fork was a good choice of weapon. It would hurt a lot and wasn't likely to seriously injure him. But you didn't use it well. A downward thrust, holding it like a dagger would have been more painful and less dangerous. I don't know if you noticed but only one of those prongs went through his skin. That's because you were just pressing thick skin into the soft fat beneath it. You got his attention though! The main thing you got right was to actually react and do something. It's not easy getting everything right when acting on impulse but a little thought about situations before you meet them can work very well. So well done, Bill. That barman will never forget you. You should be set for free beers from now on! You seem to be an impulsive chap by nature. You aren't likely to change now, so remember to get the thinking done ahead of time."

"I better had," replied Bill, who had sat mesmerised by the analysis. "Let's hope that was my swansong anyway."

"Probably won't be," said Alan, with the trace of a smile showing. "Now where has Amelia got to?"

Amelia had only rejoined them for a few minutes before it became clear that Alan needed to get going. He shook hands warmly with Bill, saying with a wink,

"Stay out of trouble old boy and keep an eye on Amelia for me, won't you? She's got a soft spot for men who get into trouble, especially older ones. It brings out her mothering instinct."

"I will do my best," he answered and returned to his chair, while the two of them said their goodbyes to each other outside. Bill heard the Toledo speeding away across the gravel.

When Amelia came back, she looked at Bill warmly and said,

"I don't know exactly what happened last night and don't need to know either. But I do know you were very brave. I feel very proud of you."

"Thank you, Amelia. I may have been more foolhardy, than brave. It's a thin line between them. I really was saved by Alan though, he appeared out of the blue just when I needed him."

"You were brave nonetheless. We shall celebrate that as well as your imminent retirement with some super champagne, as promised. After that, we need to have a chat about your next talk to the WI. I couldn't believe how much they went on about it last night."

Amelia swept out, heading for the champagne Bill supposed. As she was passing through the door, still with her back to him, he heard her saying,

"It's getting hotter than ever. I will just slip into something cooler."

When Amelia returned, Bill was feeling completely relaxed. His chair was comfortable and his mind was quiet. That all changed in a millisecond, as she bent over the coffee table to place down the tray on which rested a bottle of chilled champagne and two graceful flutes. It wasn't the champagne that had suddenly thrilled him. It was Amelia, or rather, Amelia's body. She had changed into white shorts and a chiffon blouse of pale orange. Through the blouse, Bill found himself looking at her breasts, for she was naked beneath this flimsy top. Her breasts were those of a mature, fully-formed woman, large, exquisitely curved and capped by blunt nipples. They swayed easily to her movement. He felt an intake of breath and was suddenly as enthralled as though he were a lad of fifteen.

The decision to make the change of clothing had come to her mind suddenly. It was a mixture of naughtiness, daring and curiosity that evolved quickly into action. As she felt the smoothness of the chiffon slide over her arms, she wondered how Bill would react. Would he react at all? Would he come on to her or would he react into an embarrassed protective shell? He was an unknown to her, quite perplexing and yes strangely attractive for reasons she could not define. As the chiffon settled over her, she felt a shimmering tingle as her nipples became taut.

She turned to him, smiling. "This is going to be lovely Bill. Relax and enjoy yourself. Then we will get down to business."

Bill drank his champagne readily. The swirl of gentle intoxication allowed the scene and her presence to float into a world of contentment which soon reached far beyond to a joyfulness which defied resistance.

"I congratulate you Bill, on your career and on your courage last night. I salute the talk you offered us as well and look forward to the next!"

Amelia laughed as they touched glasses and suddenly it seemed that she was a schoolgirl sitting alongside him and he was a yearning schoolboy who had just realised what beauty nature had bestowed on her. She had changed from an organising, busy person to be coped with, to a sexual creature full of mysterious unknowns.

"And I salute you too," he replied, "and thank you for the opportunities you have given me to spread my quirky ideas and also for this blissful moment."

They touched glasses once more and without further words or thoughts, they were acknowledging that suddenly, rightly or wrongly, they were sharing a moment of gentle ecstasy.

Bill didn't lose control of himself. Whilst feeling a huge privilege that this beautiful woman could be so uninhibited in front of him, he remained solidly aware that she was someone else's wife. He wondered how she really thought of him and his own seventy-year-old body. If he made a pass, it would ruin this precious time and he would never forgive himself. He decided to accept her behaviour as an exciting compliment from someone who had suddenly and unbelievably, revealed some of her sexuality as a sort of gift. He enjoyed her as she was. And she was fun.

Seeing that Bill was simply bowled over by her shape, she was enjoying him too. He was older, which she liked. He had a bit of go in him and some courage, by the sound of it. He had an interesting past and he clearly liked women. The age of his body was not on her mind. If a man was slow to respond, how delightful to help him. Oh, how much better than experiencing a painful, thrusting lover who couldn't wait to orgasm. No, this was fun, sensitive and perhaps the first of many gentle steps in a relationship that would require a little daring to fulfil. She too was experiencing happiness.

In a dream-like state, Bill found himself agreeing to do a series of Women's Institute talks on contentious issues, which he would work out one by one. He promised to do a proper question and answer session next time. He didn't remember much more of what he had agreed because Amelia had kept the champagne flowing and had also taken a quick leave of absence to return with a second bottle. He remained politely correct, if occasionally a little verbally slurred, whilst she warmed to the sight of a man responding to her body, yet keeping himself well reined in at the same time. She put on some Nat King Cole classics and let the passion trickle gently downward to a sleepy valley of warm contentment.

It was 10pm. before he felt sober enough to drive home. He didn't want to go but knew life would be better if he did.

"What will the next talk be about, dear man?" Amelia asked, as he prepared to leave.

"Drugs, dear woman, drugs!" he replied, having given the subject no thought at all.

He exited through the oaken front door and feeling steady enough, climbed into his Micra. Amelia stood, framed in the doorway, as he edged down the driveway. On his mind were that first, he hadn't done anything strictly wrong, so he could look the formidable Alan in the eye feeling sort of guilt-free the next time they met. Secondly, whatever emotions Bill was arousing in Alan's wife, they were certainly not maternal.

He just picked up her voice calling after him,

"What sort of drugs?"

"Illegal ones!" he shouted through the window.

Above the hum of the engine floated an, "Oh Jesus," comment, then he was away.

TESTICLES

Alan had mentioned the loss of a testicle almost in passing. Bill thought of this super man with downy arms as he drove himself carefully home. He resolved never to do anything untoward with his wife, come what may. Alan would never physically attack him, Bill was confident of that. He might however, be emotionally vulnerable to an under the belt advance from Bill towards his wife. Such thoughts were new to Bill and had come only after today's revealing top that Amelia had deliberately changed into and had so unexpectedly challenged him.

Alan had certainly saved him from a mauling and had possibly saved his life.

Bill had ended up losing a testicle too and the thought of it soon dragged his memories right back to the very first memory he had of his time here on earth.

It was a memory of pain. It was an intense and sick-making ache in his left groin which passed up into his abdomen. Bill didn't know how old he was when it happened but guessed he was between three and four. He recalled looking up at his mother's anxious face as she phoned urgently to the doctor. He was crouched and holding himself on the floor. By the time the doctor came, he had been put to bed and the pain had completely gone. He remembered the doctor and his mother chatting at the end of the bed. She was relaxed now and there was clearly nothing to be done. The doctor looked very important and knowledgeable.

Years later, as a medical student, Bill learned that undescended testicles can twist in early childhood, causing severe pain. If fortune smiles and they untwist spontaneously, the pain will disappear. But at that time, no one even noticed that the testicle was undescended.

Bill often wondered how in heaven's name, neither of his parents noticed that only one testicle was sitting happily in the scrotum. They must have bathed him often enough. The discovery was eventually made by a man in a tweed jacket who did the school class medical for eleven-year-olds. The system was efficient. A line of boys, naked to the waist and with trouser belts loosened, stood in front of this stranger one by one. He placed a stethoscope on the chest, said 'breathe' and then slid a hand down the front of the loosened trousers and played briefly with the scrotum.

Bill thought that was the end of it but then a letter arrived at home and Bill was told by his parents that they needed to see their own GP. No reason was given as to why and Bill, who was an accepting child, not prone to question anything in his young life, never asked. It was when the second episode of ferreting about happened that Bill began to sense where the problem might lay. This time, it was a much more painful experience of pushing and poking by his GP, that left Bill with his leg pulled up and a new wariness of doctors. Bill's dad, who had accompanied him, was not a great conversationalist and offered no explanation on the way home. Bill eventually quietly asked if everything was all right.

His father's reply stayed with Bill.

"From the waist up, you are perfectly healthy."

The conversation never progressed from there.

Later, Bill mused that even that answer had not only been uninformative but wrong. The spinal bend had yet to be noticed by anyone, as had the uneven musculature of his back. Bill himself had noticed that one shoulder was sitting higher than the other but had never questioned that either.

Another letter arrived at home and another doctor was to be visited.

Instead of calling in at the doctor's surgery, Bill's dad took him to the local hospital where a Scottish man poked Bill around even more painfully than before. There followed a long conversation between the Scottish man and Bill's dad, to which Bill was not a party. At the end, the Scottish man turned to Bill and said,

"We'll get you sorted out then, laddie."

Bill and his dad walked home in silence.

Bill was a child of his time and had assumed that others, particularly grown-up others, would know best. He began to have his first doubts whilst lying alone in the anaesthetic room waiting for an operation that he didn't understand. He was calm though, partly by nature and partly in his trust of those around him. Through the doors which led into the operating theatre were coming loud cries of pain. That was soon forgotten as the doors suddenly swung open and the same Scottish man he had seen before marched in. This time he was wearing green theatre garb, the front of which was covered in blood stains. Bill was bemused, frightened and a little excited by the surreal nature of it all. He didn't have long to ponder it though, because another stranger had appeared at his side: a woman.

"Give me your arm," said the stranger in a friendly tone of voice.

Bill watched a needle slide into a vein at his elbow and then — nothing.

The nothingness had ended. Bill found himself lying on his left side looking down at his body as nurses were mopping up blood, which appeared to be everywhere. Before any more red images were recorded, Bill found himself waking up again, back in the ward. Pain became the next memory, a gradual misery-making pain. As it rose to its very worst, a Roman Catholic priest appeared out of nowhere and started praying at the end of his bed. Bill, scarcely aware of the priest, slid a hand outside the bed, grabbed a urine bottle and after a long delay, he felt a very slow, hot flow of urine begin to trickle into it. The flow went on and on. As the prayer eventually trailed to its end, so did the flow of urine and so did most of the pain. Bill was most impressed by the effect of the prayer.

The first unguarded cough caused such a painful stab that all subsequent movements became very guarded. He hardly dared watch when the dressings were changed. The stitches had folded the skin in on itself and much worse, was the sight of his left testicle, pulled right out of the bottom of the scrotum and sewn to the top of his thigh.

No one explained what it was all about but nature set to work, healing him up. The pain slowly receded and he had his first unexpected experience of an enema, which happened unannounced one morning. After a week, he was allowed out of bed. He was so weak he fell over.

Bill's stay in hospital lasted three weeks. The second two weeks had been fun, sharing a ward with men of all ages who were fun and kind to him. Far more than this, he had time to fall in love with the nurses who tended him and touched him in special ways that no one else had ever done. His testicle slowly retracted back into the scrotum and nature miraculously healed the wounds. The operation had coincided with his sexual awakening but it had left him with baggage. Years later, when Bill was himself a doctor, he saw the same condition being treated with far less fuss. Children were being routinely operated on whilst still toddlers and done as a day case. While still a medical student, when confronted by children with the same problem as his, several times Bill found himself breaking into a sweat and needing to sit down to avoid fainting. He had never felt fully repaired and was worried he would be infertile. On one occasion, he had masturbated in the medical school toilet and had then hot-footed it to the microbiology lab, where he quickly dropped some still warm semen onto a slide, flattened it with a cover slip and then peered anxiously down at it through a powerful microscope. After some fiddling with focus and light, a fascinating scene of massive and active movement filled the lens as sperm, too many to count, wriggled with astonishing rapidity in clear view of his gaze. In spite of such clear, beautiful and dramatic evidence of full-blooded fertility, the fear of infertility continued to rest within Bill, deep and illogical. Perhaps he would be sexually inadequate too. Maybe he would set out to prove to himself he wasn't. All these thoughts and fears remained well in the background, as Bill had, almost in spite of himself, developed normal sexual desires in teenage life. His captivation with the changing shapes of teenage girls pulsed healthily through him, despite his self-inflicted doubts.

If Bill had physical problems, real or imagined, he was also well behind in his ability to socially relate to the opposite sex. His childhood had been materially well provided for but home life had been pervaded by the feeling that 'something was wrong'. It was impossible for a lad of Bill's age to work out but the problem was a breakdown in the relationship between his parents. He never experienced a life warmed and eased by hugs and kisses, holding hands, spontaneous cuddles and the affectionate ruffling of hair. Part of it was just the way of the time. The other part was the result of two parents doggedly bringing up their children in the face of shared personal disappointments and losses between each other.

'The facts of life' had been memorably presented to Bill when aged about twelve, shortly after his return home from the operation. He was carefully laying a coal fire with his dad. His newly started Boy Scout training had informed him that correct alignment of sticks was necessary to allow air to get in between, so the fire could spread. Out of the blue, slicing through his concentrated line of thought, his father said,

"In between the legs, the woman has a hole."

This was the most amazing thing ever said to Bill by his father. His hand, still clutching the sticks, froze halfway to the fireplace. An awful silence screamed between them.

'Why did he say that?' thought Bill, mentally creased and verbally paralysed with awkwardness.

It was a huge relief when his father carried uncertainly on. Looking back on it, Bill smiled at the ineffectiveness of this excruciating talk. At the end of it, he had been reassured that so long as he avoided peeing into this newly described hole, there wasn't much risk of babies growing where they weren't supposed to. Thankfully, the more advanced stuff, like eggs and sperm, never got a mention, let alone such dark concepts as erections and God forbid, desire.

In adult life, Bill came to understand his own tardiness in social development and his own hang ups. His feelings towards his parents developed more understanding and later on, he found an ever-deeper appreciation for what they had managed to give him, in spite of their own challenges.

The reality of Bill's operation was not a good result. He had developed normally sexually and in fertility but the testicle had retracted from the pinned position at the top of his thigh, to the very top of the scrotum, almost back into the groin where it had been before. There it would have remained had not Bill, in adult life, developed pain in the right testicle and sought further advice. He was in his early thirties then and was probably as fit as he ever would be but this part of his body continued to disturb him. The outcome was the removal of the left testicle as a potential malignancy risk, sitting as it was in the wrong position (a risk that later came to be regarded as minimal or non-existent), plus the removal of a harmless cyst that had twisted and caused pain on the right side. The left testicle was replaced by a silicone prosthesis which gave Bill the simple pleasure of looking entirely normal. It also gave him an appreciation for the psychological difficulties of others for what, to an outsider, appeared minor problems.

Bill knew several men who had one testicle. Alan was the latest. Two he knew had developed testicular cancer but both had survived. Two had lost theirs due to trauma, though not as dramatic as Alan's trauma, and one to infection. None of them seemed impaired outwardly in any way, though they had all had their own journeys no doubt. Bill put his heavy weather approach down to the failure of communication between himself as an eleven-year-old, his parents and the doctors. Now, aged seventy, what had happened had happened and that was that. He had put it all to rest. Not only was he a healthy seventy-year-old, albeit feeling over tired, he had had some memorable sexual experiences, he had three fantastic children and someone was again showing him that his remaining sexual embers had not been extinguished. He resolved not to make trouble for anyone, himself included, as a result of the recent fanning of those erotic embers.

It had been a long tale of woe for Bill. To meet someone like Alan, whose testicle had been shot away in an instant and who appeared impressively unfazed about it, was a boost for him. If Alan could be like that about it, then he could be too.

THE SECOND WOMEN'S INSTITUTE TALK

Amelia phoned.

"Hello Bill. Are you okay?" without waiting for an answer she went on, "I have put your name down as the speaker for next Wednesday and have said that you are doing a short series of talks for us, designed to make us all think a bit. Is that fair, Bill? I hope so. Now, while I have you, Mrs Carantoc, you know, the lady right at the front close to you with the thick glasses? Well, she nearly had a heart attack when you banged the table Bill, so can you cut that sort of thing out please? Poor Mrs Carantoc doesn't see at all well and wasn't expecting such a thump right in front of her. Other than that, people have been talking about what you had to say. I can't imagine anyone actually doing anything about it, but it did get us talking. One person who did agree with you wholeheartedly was Alan. I believe he has spent some time there in the past. You can talk to him about it sometime."

"When does he get back?" Bill asked.

"I never know, so can't tell you but he's not usually away more than a month. Work is probably doing him good at the moment. He's had some other problems, nothing to do with work and it helps him get back on track. That's my feeling anyway. He'll tell you sometime, I'm sure."

"Okay Amelia," replied Bill, resisting the urge to probe, "and how are you?"

"I'm in good shape," she said.

"That's nice to hear. It's unusual to hear women say that, you know. There is generally something amiss, usually something to do with their shape!"

"Oh, tish tosh!" she exclaimed. "The shape I am is the shape it is and if anyone doesn't like it, that's their problem, not mine!"

"Quite right," agreed Bill knowing full well that if ever there was an admirer of her shape, it was him. "Well thanks for checking up about the talk. I'll see you there same as before and I promise not to scare the audience."

"Bless you, Bill. You are an absolute darling doing this you know. I am so grateful."

Bill felt some surprise over her vagueness about Alan's work. She didn't even seem sure if he had been working in Northern Ireland or not. He wondered if his non-work problems were between the two of them. Once again, he vowed not to rock the boat.

On the evening of the talk, he again made his way to the Red Lion, on his way to the WI hall. Martin greeted him cheerfully at the bar, spotting him as soon as he entered.

"Hello trouble! Hell, you've made a bit of a name for yourself Bill. Let's keep it gentle from now on, eh?"

"I wasn't spoiling for a fight exactly," replied Bill, "but no more shenanigans tonight! Anyway, my guardian angel is away."

The pub was only about half full, as dictated by the Covid restrictions. It was enough to create an ambience and it also left Martin more time than usual to chat with Bill. He departed briefly to tend the fire with cut logs, that occasionally spat sparks harmlessly onto the slate hearth. On returning he asked Bill,

"What are you going to light up the evening with tonight then Bill? Another dose of 'When I was in the Congo'?"

"No, I've done all that. In fact, there's nothing left to say any more about my medical escapades abroad. The ladies are a bright lot you know. There's no way I would get away with the same old stories going around again. It's a brand-new subject this evening Martin, drugs, including the legal ones like yours."

"Hah!" snorted Martin. "We should ban the lot of them and put the dealers away for life."

"The way I see the issue Martin, that would be very bad for a business like yours."

"Bollocks!" retorted Martin, "there's no comparing a decent trade like this to the shit going on in the streets."

"I think you should come to the talk. Maybe I can make you feel differently," Bill smiled. Martin was reassuringly predictable in many of his opinions. Whilst Bill's own opinions were often far away from mainstream, he was refreshingly free of any need for others to agree with him. He was always pleased however, when he observed that someone had really thought for themselves about any issue at all.

"You won't change me old boy. There's right and wrong and you bloody well know it!"

When Bill left the pub to make his way down to the WI hall, he was still rolling around in his mind how exactly to deliver the presentation. After his chat with Martin, he felt the evening could be an interesting one.

Amelia was on door duty again and delivered another blow to his forearm and the warmest of smiles.

"Back again, Dr Smith, how time flies! You had quite an effect on us last time, so heaven knows what you will be up to this evening! Do go in Doctor, you are on first again, we will start in about ten minutes."

The all-female audience was spaced as before. At the allotted moment, Bill rose to the podium and as an expectant hush fell, he began his talk.

"Good evening, ladies," he began.

"I am going to tell you some stories and go over some simple, well-known facts and then I want you all to ask yourselves what you, as an individual, think about the issues concerned. I am not asking any of you to do anything but it is possible that someone here might want to. I don't mind."

He paused to assess his listeners. Yes, they were all there with him. He continued.

"Back in 1927, in America, a successful businessman called Wilson Hickox from Cleveland, Ohio, took an alcoholic nightcap to unwind after a busy day. A few minutes later, he was dead. His age was forty-three. His death would have been painful and frightening. He had been poisoned, by strychnine. His alcoholic nightcap had been spiked by deadly poison.

"Who had done this dastardly thing? Well, surprisingly, it was the American government. They were anxious to protect their citizens from the evils of alcohol; so anxious it seems, that murdering a few of them seemed the best way forward at the time, thereby warning the masses off the awful drink. Sadly, such acts rest today like unremembered dust, no longer warning us of how enthusiastic a government can be in its efforts to protect us. The difficulty in banning alcohol is that it was essential and still is, for tasks such as thinning paint, antifreezes, antiseptics among others. It wasn't possible to eliminate it from usage all together, so to prevent it being misused, that is being drunk, alcohol of all sorts was poisoned; or to use the politically correct parlance of the time, denatured.

"This policy left a yawning gap in the drinks market for figures such as Al Capone, who had no desire to slight the opportunity. He was soon providing alcoholic beverages which lacked the troublesome side-effect of causing sudden death. In one report (in 'Eating in America' by Root and De Rochemont), it is estimated that up to eleven thousand people died in America from poisoning in this manner in the year of 1927 alone. This was at the hands of a State that was supposed to be looking after its people. In a master stroke, the government shut down the legitimate drinks industry worth about two billion dollars a year and presented it to the murderous thugs of the time. You will find all this publicised in Bill Bryson's book about one Summer in America, in 1927.

"I tell you this little story because in hindsight, most of us today would say that the American government had been wrong. So now, let us be a little more questioning about what our present-day government is doing here in the UK, right now.

"When I qualified as a young doctor, my first job was with a consultant who happened to be the Queen's Physician. This was back in the 1970s, and he was already nearing retirement. He was a man of character and wisdom. He told us the tale of two young nurses who had just come off their first ever night shift. They were trainees and it was before the war. There were no restrictions on addictive drugs such as we now have. So, they helped themselves to a shot of heroine each, to ensure they got off to sleep. One of them never touched the drug again and the other was addicted for life. The point my physician boss went on to make was that both of them worked out full careers as nurses. The addicted one was kept supplied by her GP, who was also unfettered by regulation and gave her a reliable supply of clean drugs and needles. Heroine that is unpolluted, is extremely addictive but nowhere near as dangerous as we are led to believe.

"Clean heroine is less risky than excessive alcohol and regular cigarettes. It doesn't seem like that, because we have given the trade to criminals. The current illegal scene is one of dangerously varying drug strengths, which may or may not be contaminated. There is a constant risk of accidental overdose. The stuff is then injected by potentially disease-ridden equipment. The whole sordid scene is financed by rampant crime. The money comes from the likes of you and me, as and when we are robbed.

"The actual cost of a shot of heroine is less than a pound. Make it illegal and you can multiply that sum by a hundred. And who gets the profit?"

A murmur passed through the room.

"Do you remember that last time I told you that we humans generate our responses from either a loving background, or a fearful background? Here you can see the fear at work: who wants a society full of drugged up zombies, incapable of decent behaviour? Well, surprisingly, most people want to live a healthy and fulfilled life. Those that do opt for drugs won't be the mountaineers, the surgeons, or the politicians of the world. They will have opted for their own style and will pay the consequences. However, if they want to head downhill in their lives, do we want them to pull society down with them — by their endless need to rob and steal?

"What about a less fearful reaction, a bit more loving perhaps? Well, we don't want to tell people how to live their lives, unless they are hurting others — which of course drug addicts do all the time at the moment. They have made their choice. However, the scene could be made safe, affordable, and a modest tax on legal drugs would allow rehabilitation centres to operate for those that wish to get clean altogether. Someone that causes harm as a result of taking drugs would deserve full punishment. We do that already with drunken drivers, do we not?

"You see the whole conundrum pivots on who is responsible for the problem: the producer, or the consumer."

Bill stopped for another look around the room. There was a little restlessness but their attention was still with him. He knew he mustn't drone on. His mind quickly fashioned an end point.

"Have any of you visited the lovely Scottish Isle of Islay?"

"Yes, I have," spoke out a lady at the front with thick glasses, who Bill surmised must be Mrs Carantoc.

"Do you remember anything about their local industry there?"

"Yes indeed," she replied unhesitatingly "It's whisky, whisky, whisky!"

"Exactly," said Bill. "I visited there a couple of years ago. It is a beautiful island and dotted around I counted eight distilleries and two more were being built. Over there, whisky is a serious investment and the different flavours are admired the world over.

"Now, if an alcoholic stumbles into hospital clutching a

bottle of best Islay whisky, should we send the police around to destroy the distilleries that produce such noxious stuff?

"No, of course not. Everyone realises, including the alcoholic, that they have the problem and they are responsible. If they keep drinking then they will take the consequences." Bill was careful not to shout this time.

"And that, ladies, is my simple point to you for this evening. Responsibility lies with the consumer, not the producer. When a drug is legalised, the recognition of the user's responsibility happens automatically. When it is criminalised, the user will never feel responsible for their own actions. They feel like victims and don't own their problem"

Bill paused, feeling he had made his point and had not droned on for too long.

"Does anyone wish to make a point or air a view on this? After all, it can affect anyone of us in terms of being robbed. Maybe some of our children or grand-children are at risk of being sucked into taking drugs. It is everyone's problem."

A voice, clear and articulate, came from the centre of the room.

"Doctor, are you, as a medical man, saying that we should allow all drugs to be used by anyone at any time?"

"Thanks for that question. No, I am not. In a couple of instances regarding drugs, I feel that our government has it as good as possible already. I mean specifically alcohol and tobacco. There are age restrictions on their usage which to me are appropriate. In addition, the information about the harm they can cause is well and truly out there. No one doubts that cigarettes increase the risk of lung cancer. It is left to us, as individuals, to decide if we want to accept that risk, or not. The approach taken on those two drugs would be my basis for all others."

"Well, I think the world would be a better place if all drug addicts were put in prison and dealers for twice as long." came the retort.

"That is the basic aim of current regulations, isn't it?" said Bill. "If it was working, I would be happy enough with that myself. But and this is big but and why we all have to think about it, do you think the current situation is working?"

"Well, it's better than just accepting defeat I say. I won't give in to those criminals."

"Fair enough," replied Bill gently. "But here is the general point about decision making that perhaps we all should all consider.

"The question is not, is something right or wrong? The question to ask is, does this work for us? If it doesn't, how can we make it work? Remember that right and wrong change with the fashion of the day, sometimes very quickly. Alcohol was wrong in America at one stage, now it is accepted. Which regime works best? How many of you think that the system we have now is working for us?"

No hands rose.

"So," Bill added, "our job is to find out what does"

"Anyone taking drugs should be put in prison," came another voice from the back, a voice tinged with anger.

"Okay," said Bill "At least you are coming up with how you feel, though I will always ask you to keep asking yourself if something in place is actually working. Now, in response to your point, are you saying for example, that anyone who takes say, cocaine, should be imprisoned."

"That is exactly what I am saying," came back the voice and Bill could now dimly make out a lady leaning towards him through the gloom.

"Well, why not try reading the autobiographies of Elton John and Stephen Fry. They both describe, in detail the results of prolonged cocaine sniffing. They both seem to be free of the habit now, mainly because they were able to own the problem and accept their own responsibility in becoming clean. Importantly, they were both wealthy enough to pay for the help they needed. But they are as guilty as the devil's wand with regard to having used it. Would the world be a better place if they were put in jail? Is that what you think we should do with such illustrious sinners, or is it just non-celebrities, the lesser folk, we should imprison?"

"Oh, don't be ridiculous!"

Bill laughed.

"It's not easy, is it? Nothing is black and white. Think about it ladies. Remember to ask, is this working for you? Is it working for us? Is it working for our country? If it is, leave it alone. If it isn't, what can be done to change it? I am not asking any of you to go out and change the world but I am asking you all to open your minds to this and any other problem.

"I will be offering you a different one to ponder next time.

Ladies, thank you all very much."

The applause was polite rather than enthusiastic and Bill could hear Amelia's clapping above the lot of them.

He suddenly felt a bit weary and so headed through the room which was now abuzz with chatter, towards the door. Amelia was engaged in conversation with a group of people but called out as he was passing.

"Doctor, I haven't thanked you! Oh, never mind, too late! Thank you anyway! I need to talk to you when I can, Doctor. Not now, we are just about to get going with the business section. Would you mind calling me when you are free?"

"No worries," he called back. "Thanks for this evening, Amelia. Bye!"

He looked at her briefly but closely as he spoke. She was animated, happy looking and smart too. Her hair was brushed back and held in place by a flowered head band. Her blue eyes sparkled. A loose, rose-coloured cardigan, with a distinct home-made look about it, lay comfortably about her.

Bill was pleased to get into the fresh, night air. He decided not to go to the pub again but walked steadily towards home while his thoughts lingered on Amelia. He had been thrilled by the sight of herself that she had offered him. His anxiety over her behaviour and his reaction to her was unaltered. There was no way he was going to get into any gap between her and Alan. Just no! But, he pondered, suppose Alan wasn't in the picture. Why would a beautiful and confident woman like Amelia show any amorous interest in him? He was physically a fairly normal-looking, seventy-year-old man and she was a woman in her mature prime. He guessed her age to be similar to Alan's. She could practically choose any partner she wanted. He didn't think his intellect would suffice to entice her interest in his direction, any more than his body would. It was odd, if flattering. Maybe she was just playing with him. It didn't feel like that; he had detected a genuine warmth. Anyway, none of it mattered because Alan was on the scene, so that was that. He tried to roll his thoughts away from Amelia.

The summer evening had chilled a little and thick clouds had blotted out the evening stars. A fine drizzle covered his face with a watery down of droplets. He felt enervated by the moisture. To keep his wandering thoughts in line, he amused himself by admiring the patterns of drizzle that shone around the street lights, as tiny tuffets of breeze set off a swirling dance between the water and air and highlighted it in the orange spotlights.

By considerable effort of will, Bill waited two days before calling her.

"Hi Amelia, Bill reporting in."

"Oh, hello Bill. Thank you so much for getting back to me. Your talk got everyone going again. It was really jolly good fun in the end, with various groups forming and people getting rather aerated about it all. Bill you are a stirrer on the quiet, you know. You say your bit and then, as the reaction begins to heat up, you slip off down the pub!"

"Well, I didn't go to the pub actually. I just strolled home, enjoying the night air."

"Well, that's quite an improvement on what happened last time. I still can't believe that Alan happened to be there just at the right time like that."

"Lady luck smiled on me, that's for sure. When is he getting back? Does he communicate while he is away?"

"Sometimes he does. Often not. Usually, he just re-appears on the door step. He's generally a bit tired when he gets home but he doesn't let on what he's been up to. It's not a good set-up for anyone really."

Bill's opinion of what the problem was firmed a little in his mind.

Amelia continued,

"I am in the middle of planning the next few Women's Institute activities, including your talks. Why don't you choose a good day and come around for coffee so we can talk it over.

You said you had run out of ideas before and then you came up with Northern Ireland and now drugs, which you clearly want to make available to the whole world! You are quite unpredictable you know, maybe even dangerous. Have you thought you might be dangerous, Bill? I want to quiz you a bit before setting you loose on my unsuspecting flock again!"

"I'm not the slightest bit dangerous," he protested, but he gave in to her coffee invitation with no resistance. The following day suited both of them.

Bill was beginning to feel less tired. His night-time work for CCAS had come to an end and the improved sleep was showing results. The stimulation of Amelia was also helping and he was pleased that, even though it was impossible for the situation to honourably progress, he had felt his body and emotions respond. He wasn't feeling completely right though. His desire to run flickered but he wasn't feeling the usual uninhibited desire to get out and away. He sensed that a few miles running would still leave a prolonged feeling of fatigue, instead of a physical and mental boost. Nonetheless, overall things were marginally better. He must be patient. This time he allowed the thought to briefly pass through his mind that he was, actually, seventy years old.

And then the dentist phoned. They were back working but the Personal Protective Equipment required and cleaning of equipment between patients meant a gap of between one and two hours was required between each one. However, they could fit Bill in at 9am. the next day. Bill was happy to accept. He couldn't wait to get rid of the damned plate and get the front tooth bridge completed. That would get him feeling more normal, more presentable, younger even!

He turned up punctually, hidden behind his required face

covering and, after mandatory hand sanitisation, he was led into the dentist's surgery where his attractive lady dentist and her assistant were scarcely recognisable behind eye visors, face masks and sheets of plastic covering their bodies.

'What a miserable way to work,' thought Bill. But he settled for giving a cheery greeting to them both, before submitting to their skilled and efficient attentions.

He was fixed up in a mere twenty minutes and left with more than enough time to get to Amelia's. She would be preparing coffee for 11am.

'It's not viable,' he thought to himself. 'Working all trussed up like that.' He felt a genuine concern for the people who had just attended to him.

He reviewed the Covid-19 situation that he had gleaned from the press and TV. As he understood it, there was currently one case for every seventeen hundred people in England. Local hotspots had been shut down again. That seemed sensible, he thought. The death rate seemed to be around one in a thousand cases, mainly concentrated in people aged over seventy and younger ones who were overweight or who had various debilitating conditions. The hospitals had worked hard with the serious cases and hadn't been overwhelmed. Bill had joined in the Thursday evening clap for the NHS. His own contribution felt miniscule in comparison to the intensive care hospital staff. The virus could certainly bite hard and healthy-looking people, including doctors and nurses, had also died.

Bill was interested to hear that the nose and throat swab test for the virus could now be completed in ninety minutes and the facilities to do the test were transportable. Since then, talk of a saliva test had popped up. There were a few spare minutes before he needed to set off to Amelia's, so he Googled it to take a look. It seemed that it could be more reliable to have someone spit into a container than to half-heartedly poke a cotton bud up their nose and around the gaggy bit of their throat. The pick-up rate was clearly still uncertain but the actual test could now be done in fifteen minutes. Could this be true? Perhaps, he mused, the answer was to get a mobile lab to the centre of every town. Then, when one needed to go to the dentist, or get on a train, the test could be done immediately beforehand and some sort of negative certificate would allow the person to be treated reasonably normally. The tests could also be done before allowing passengers to enter a cruise terminal. Airport terminals could only allow negative testers in, the test being done immediately prior to any flight, right outside the terminal. At least everyone on the flight would know that the person sitting next to them had also just had a negative test.

Bill wasn't sure what the level of false negatives really was but the recent rapid and more mobile testing facility should help open things up soon. One thing was for sure, those dental people needed some help. He resolved to write to them expressing his appreciation for what they had done for him.

All such thoughts faded from his mind as he drove slowly up the gravel drive to the big, oak door of Amelia's home.

She opened the door beaming a healthy, welcoming smile and within seconds, Bill found himself enveloped in her arms. She was about five feet eight inches tall, judging by his own height of six feet and Bill found his cheek resting against her hair. She smelled wholesome and felt warm. He found himself raising a hand to press her head towards him but stopped himself. The hug lasted just a little longer than it should have but not so long as to require explanation to each other, or anyone else, though it left Bill's mind racing and his pulse quickened.

Releasing him, Amelia led the way into the lounge, where from the window, Bill spotted the rim of a swimming pool which he had not previously noticed. Amelia, having positioned Bill in a comfortable chair with a garden view which revealed more of the pool, left the room to fetch coffee and biscuits. This time there were healthy alternatives to the biscuits, in the form of grapes and sliced kiwi fruit, both of which Bill enjoyed. He was relieved that Amelia was wearing a light top that wasn't transparent. Her company was enough for him and he didn't want to spoil what was turning into a fabulous relationship by falling over that sensitive line that defines all such relationships. Not only that, he realised he was a little scared at the prospect anyway. Talking, sharing food, making plans for the WI talks were all safe, so why risk it all? There was also the unmentioned factor of Alan.

"Well Bill, how are you?"

"I'm good thanks Amelia," he answered. "In fact, better than I have been for a while. I was feeling generally a bit knackered so have been taking life a bit more easily. I can feel some energy coming back."

"You're not ill, are you? You look well, I must say. But you men are simply dreadful at looking after yourselves. Alan comes home sometimes completely exhausted and pretends he is normal, and I can see that he isn't. Mind you, a bit like you I suppose, he seems to bob up quickly enough. How have you been overdoing it anyway? Are these WI talks a bit too dangereuse?" She burst out laughing and he smiled back.

"No, the WI talks are fine. I am enjoying getting stuff off

my chest, that I have been boring friends about for years. No, it's a build-up of stuff I have been doing over many years, just slightly overdoing things day after day without even really noticing it. I've had to take stock of myself recently, because suddenly the things I have enjoyed for ages became, well, not exactly unpleasurable but exhausting. There was no particular reason but when I thought about life over the last ten years, since I got divorced in fact, I could see how I have been pushing things to a greater or lesser extent. So I am being firm with myself. No more early morning runs, for the time being anyway. I indulge in lay-ins and exercise only when I really fancy it."

"Ooh, lovely!" She flicked a smile across to him and he knew that if anyone could get him out of the doldrums, it was her.

"Well, I am glad it's not the WI talks doing the damage," she continued, "because they want some more from you and I need to tell them how many more we are planning. Your subjects are different to the usual sort of thing we have. Normally we go for interest subjects, or hobbies, or slide shows. Now Bill, how many more subjects are lurking in that devious mind of yours? I have to start planning for them you see and then beyond."

"Well, for the next one I was going to talk about the Syrian refugee problem and what I feel we should have done about it and probably still could. Then, there is the background to Brexit and I want to add in an idea about a little constitutional change to bolster up the running of Parliament. After all, we were the laughing stock of the world with all our indecision about Brexit. Everyone was saying that Parliament wasn't fit for service and now it's going on exactly the same as ever."

"Wow, you'll find some sore tempers over Brexit all right. Good luck anyway. I won't try and advise you. That would be, how shall I put it, non-productive. I am learning about you Bill and there is more to you than is first apparent, most of it quite endearing."

She flashed her smile at him. He suddenly noticed the fullness of her lips. She wore no make-up. He loved the naturalness of her. There was something almost feline about her. He wanted to stroke her.

"I will tell the committee then," she said." Do you have any other burning topics?"

"That will do I think," replied Bill. "That's four altogether and they will probably be keen to move on after that." Bill sat back in his comfortable chair before continuing. "I have enjoyed doing the first two talks Amelia, mainly because the audience has reacted. There has been a buzz of conversation as I slip away. I like that you know. When I talk to family and friends about what to me are important issues, I am sometimes almost shocked that they don't seem to have thought about the problem at all. And if they have, then they regard it as someone else's problem and nothing to do with them."

"I expect family and friends want something different from you Bill and you have probably been boring them silly for years!"

"Well," he responded "I haven't touched on the meaning of life, and why we are all here, have I? Just be grateful for that!"

She laughed. "Okay, Bill, I am grateful."

She gave him a little grin. "You can tell me. But not now though, because there is something I want to tell you."

She swung around in her chair to face him directly.

"Here, come with me, I'll tell you about it in the garden."

Outside, the air was warm and patchily scented with rose and honeysuckle. French windows led onto a patio. The back garden was spacious and south facing, so the sunshine was at that moment direct, with only the gentlest of breezes to temper it. It was late summer, so whilst flowers dotted the scene with colour, the ground was littered with petals and leaves. Areas of rabbit droppings were tucked under rose bushes and crocosmia had spread randomly, spiking the air with its vivid orange and yellow flowers. From the patio, a curved path led to the pool, which was both rippling and enticing. Smooth slabs bordered the pool itself, whilst beyond the slabs was lawn. Flowerbeds surrounded the lawn and behind them, a mixture of large shrubs and small trees gave the garden a special and exquisite sense of privacy. A breath of wind gossiped with the leaves. In the distance came the hollow barking of a dog.

"Take my hand Bill. I want to talk to you about something special. It's not something you can talk to many people about, because people are just so, oh I don't know, judgemental, I suppose, is what I am trying to say."

She offered her hand and Bill took it, gently caressing her fingers. Suddenly she was needing some reassurance herself.

"We can sit over there."

She led the way to a traditional conversation chair, a wooden pair of seats angled slightly towards each other and joined together by a narrow flat surface ideal for resting a glass of wine on, whilst enjoying conversation and the garden ambience with a partner.

"Are you okay here Bill? You aren't too hot?"

Bill, a master of dealing with the dangers of hot sunshine on his bald head, had already slipped a baseball cap out of his pocket and put it on. He was feeling not only comfortable in the sunshine but had completely surrendered to the charms of the beautiful creature beside him; such that "happy" was not word enough to describe his mood.

"Have you heard of Tantric sex?"

"I have heard of it, yes," he replied, "but can tell you virtually nothing about it."

"Well Bill, I am not an expert. But I will tell you what I think it means. I have been to some of their weekend sessions you see. There's nothing secret about it. Anyone who is interested can look them up online. They cost a lot and are bloody scary. At least, to start with they're scary. Once you get to understand what they are on about it's not too bad. By the time you reach the end of one of their sessions, you begin to realise that they are telling you something really important."

"Did Alan go with you?"

"Alan? Good God no, never even told him."

Bill decided not to pursue it but felt a ripple of anxiety wriggle into his euphoria.

"The gist of it is this," Amelia went on, completely unfazed by Bill's mention of Alan. "Sex to many of us, is the best, most exciting and fulfilling experience that we will experience in our lifetime. That doesn't apply to everyone but it does to many. For lots of us it goes wrong, for a myriad of reasons. Right now, there are loads of kids whose main instruction comes from online pornography. So pretty girls shave themselves and get awful things injected into their lips, so they pout like goldfish. The boys see aggressive sex, with no male role models showing them things like respect and tenderness for their partner, or even enjoyment for themselves. There are some though, who get it right. These people may have just been lucky, or may have been able to work their own way out of tradition and religious dictates that can be so damaging. The thing is, they get to those high places of sexual joy, which in turn leads to a space of spiritual joy. It is like the pleasure of sharing a great conversation with someone, or a meal with an old friend but a million times better and much, much closer. People who find this place are set to spread their own happiness into the world. They have confidence from the actual experience, that life in this world can be truly wonderful. Their demeanour and activities are enhanced long after the sexual act that set them up there. People like that actually make the world a better place.

"Tantra is about showing ordinary people how to get there. There is a physical or sexual side to what they teach and the reward is felt in the rest of life. Spiritual enhancement is the best way I can describe it to you. Some say they feel closer to God but you don't need to be religious to feel it."

She paused and squeezed his hand. Bill found himself thinking back to the woman who had once flushed and groaned beneath him. He felt then and had even said to her at the time, that something eternal had happened.

Amelia carried on,

"Some people who go to the Tantra sessions are married couples. They can go on their own if they want. At the sessions I went to, we were a mix of individuals, some married, some not. They were all sorts of ages. There was one woman there aged seventy-four whose fifty-year-old marriage had continued only because of an affair with another man that she was still having, which had started forty years ago. She said she loved both men. Sex does happen but not for quite a while. There is a lot of talking about why we are there, the things that went wrong and for most of us, the list seemed quite long. I got to admire lots of people who were striking out in spite of all sorts of negative experiences they had had. I suppose that's what had turned them to Tantra in the first place. The main impressions I got, were that the men were incredibly sensitive creatures with far more anxiety that you would have believed. The size of their penis, the shape of their balls, whether or not they had an erection. God, they went on and on about stuff that we women weren't expecting at all. They certainly weren't the wham, bang, thank you mam brigade! What the men said to us as women though, was sometimes really lovely. They were amazed how beautiful an ordinary woman could suddenly appear in their eyes. They were often incredibly kind and flattering. All the stuff that women go on about, like their boobs, or their weight, didn't seem to matter. What they really were after was someone who just, well, I don't know really, just responded to them.

"Before any sexual activity started, they explained to us the philosophy of it all. Firstly, there was an acceptance that the very best was a couple who shared their sex life together and spread their joy from it to the rest of the world but it wasn't the only way. That is the whole point of Tantra. Mixing together as virtual strangers as we were, we had the usual talk about sexual health and so on but our relationship had to be one of mutual trust. You and your Tantra partner were to learn together in a safe place, giving respect to each other for sharing such an intimate learning process. What actually happened between couples was always an unknown. One couple I remember just didn't fancy each other sexually, so instead of laying down together, they shared a walk and had a cup of tea. That was as highly regarded as those that went all the way sexually. No one did anything they didn't want to do and there was a lot of asking permission about stuff, which always felt a bit odd. With guidance and reassurance mainly, some couples began to really get it together. It was the first time I had ever heard adults giving honest sexual accounts of themselves. Just occasionally, relationships developed which continued beyond the supervised sessions. It was important to follow the Tantra Mantra, that we were there to share, help and respect each other. If one of the pair was married and wanted to give all their sex back to their partner, then the Tantra partner was to thank them for their help and wish them well in their future journey. I don't expect it always worked out quite as angelically as that but you can see what they were saying. I never saw it happen but there must have been some relationships from those groups that evolved into marriages. The only case I know where that had happened was the couple who actually ran the group. They had met doing some kind of sex work, started a Tantra group and ended up getting married."

Amelia, stopped talking. She looked Bill straight in the eye. He was feeling warmed by the beauty of her and saw sincerity in her eyes. She had spoken with feeling and earnestness.

"I trust you, Bill. You are a decent man. I am going to get us both a glass of wine. Think about it while I am fetching it. I am asking you to be my Tantric partner."

She left him gazing across the lawn and into the blue sky beyond. The distant sound of a door being pushed open broke into his reverie. Faintly but clearly, he heard Amelia saying,

"Alan, you're back!"

Bill felt himself emotionally reeling as though from a

body punch. Had Amelia really said all that to him, or were they just the vagaries of an ailing old man? He felt bewildered beyond description. No time to brood though.

"Bill! Good to see you."

Alan was striding towards him across the grass, arm in arm with Amelia who was smiling happily.

"Good to see you too," Bill lied back.

Amelia turned smiling to Alan saying,

"You are absolutely hopeless Alan. You never tell me when to expect you. Bill and I were right in the middle of something important."

'Christ!' thought Bill.

"Look," answered Alan, "I am under orders for far too much of the time as it is. I'm damned if I am going to start taking orders from you too! Anyway, this place is as much mine as yours. I can turn up whenever I want"

Amelia turned to Bill, still looking confident and entirely relaxed. "We inherited this place from our mum, three years ago." She said, "We spent the last few years of our time at home here, so we both like it too much to let the other have it as their own."

OUR mum, the brown hair, the blue eyes, the facial look — suddenly it was all so mind-blowingly obvious.

Bill cursed his own awe-inspiring imbecility and suddenly found himself beaming at the brother and sister standing before him.

Ignoring the change in Bill's expression, Amelia continued,

"Alan's wife died just a few months back, so this is a kind of rest and recuperation station for him while he gets his feet back on the ground. I live here all the time now and plan to stay."

"Oh, I see." A vague light-headedness came over Bill. He knew he should leave.

"Look," he said, "I am going to leave you two to it. You need to catch up on things. Thanks for a great chat, Amelia, and I'll give you a call very soon."

He became firm in words and actions as he knew some protestations about his departure were close, especially from Alan but he needed to go. He offered his hand to Alan who shook it warmly and to Amelia he gave his first ever uninhibited hug, which lifted her feet an inch clear of the ground. It was a clear non-verbal yes answer to her question, which he would look forward to expressing verbally later when they would be speaking alone. The nature of the hug was not wasted on Alan, who said smilingly as Amelia regained contact with the earth,

"I might be able to help you in a scrap Bill but if you tangle with her, you're on your own!"

He ducked, as his sister swung an arm at him. Bill found the door, still bewildered by the sudden aggregate of forces to such positive happiness that had engulfed him.

The next day, Bill wandered down to the Red Lion. Business was ticking over nicely in spite of the Covid restrictions and Martin was seeming happy enough. Bill had phoned Amelia that morning and had come off the phone with instructions to get an all clear from the local sexually transmitted disease clinic. This had both surprised and pleased him, as he was in no doubt that she would be doing the same. He could hardly believe what he was about. He had also listened to some of her family history, which included the fact that she was still having periods. Pregnancy was not a risk however because she had been sterilised after the birth of her second child. Amelia had a son and a daughter. Further enquiries elicited that the children were now in their mid-twenties and both lived far from home. Their father had also been a military man, like Alan. He had been killed in some kind of military accident. Amelia had changed back to her maiden name after his death. She didn't describe their relationship more deeply and there was far more to learn about her but the bones of her life story had been displayed to him. She had told him the beginnings of her story with a matter of factness that simply ramped up his feeling of how divinely beautiful she was.

Martin wandered across, carrying a full glass of Doom Bar which he placed in front of Bill.

"On the house," he declared.

He was looking slightly different to normal. A checkered neckerchief circled his neck. Bill thought it would make a good handle to grab but Martin was ahead of him.

"If anybody grabs this Bill, my friend, this is how you get them off."

Martin pushed his forearms together and upwards under his neck and then strongly outwards.

"I started Tae Kwando last night," he said, "so next time I will have some hope of looking after myself."

"Very good," said Bill. He liked the look of the neckerchief. It made Martin look interesting. He went on,

"You sound a bit like me. I was badly frightened by a drug addict in the surgery once. Drug addicts can be inveterate liars, so what they say doesn't always mean very much. He was just desperate for drugs and people like that can lose it very quickly."

"Did he go for you then?" asked Martin.

"No but he scared the shit out of me. It's what sent me to a Tae Kwando club just the same as you."

"How did the Tae Kwando go? Did it help? Would you have dealt with that fat guy who grabbed me without the help of the other chap?"

"Tae Kwando is Korean for 'The Art of Hand and Foot'. What I learned wasn't at all what I expected to learn. In answer to your question, no, I was in trouble Martin. What I had already learned from Tae Kwando is that an attack by someone with a knife is hard to defend against. We used to practise it using plastic knives and I always got stabbed."

"Jesus Christ! I didn't even know he had a knife."

"Well, I had spotted that much. He was just reaching down for it when my saviour spoke up. I know a bit more about him now by the way. He is in the military with some sort of Special Services. He's Amelia Cordite's brother, Alan Cordite." Bill tried to sound casual about it. "I met up with him recently at Amelia's. We were discussing the WI talks, when he came in and gave me some tips on how I should have looked after myself better."

"Well, you saved my bacon and he saved yours, by the sound of it. Funny that he didn't even move a muscle though! So tell me Bill, how far did you get with Tae Kwando and was it worthwhile? Most of the students at the club I have joined are really young. They have a beginners' group for an hour, with loads of children. That's where I am of course and I feel a right Grandpa, I can tell you. Then, a more advanced group comes in for a second hour. Some of them look a bit grizzly."

"Well," replied Bill, "I had several injuries in training but only some of them were fatal."

"Bloody idiot, how did you get hurt in training? You, dipstick, you."

"Well, three hits on three different occasions caused some damage. The fist was when the instructor was demonstrating how to strike someone using the knee. Knees and elbows are very powerful weapons, Martin. Anyway, he did a mock punch to my stomach. I bent over as per the plan but bent too far and had a real contact with his knee."

"Did it hurt?"

"It broke my nose. The gush of blood was quite spectacular and the other students, who were mainly teenagers, were most impressed."

"I bet they were! Did you need any treatment?"

"Well, I was working the next day and went around impressing all my patients with baggy, blood-filled pouches under both eyes. I wasn't in any real pain and kept forgetting what I looked like. I was examining a lady's sprained ankle in the local Minor Injuries Unit and she thought I was another patient, casually touching her up. It was my fault for not properly introducing myself and explaining the ghastly appearance. Fortunately, the nurse calmed her down okay and explained to her what I should have explained beforehand."

"Bill, you are a right plonker sometimes. I don't know how you lasted out a career in medicine. But did your nose need any treatment?"

"I went to an ENT chap, who went on and on about a deviated septum, hypertrophy of inferior turbinate bones and so on. He ended up proposing major sounding surgery, so I said thanks but no thanks. It has left me with a crooked nose with the bone indented here."

Bill pointed to the prominent bump on one side of his nose

with a depression lying on the other side. "Afterwards, I cursed myself for not elevating the depressed bit of bone myself. It would have been easy enough using something like a toothbrush handle. I read about an Australian rugby player called Weary Dunlop doing exactly that. He was a doctor too. By the time I thought of it, the time had passed. Still, the only problem I get now is a sore nose on one side from glasses, otherwise all is whoopeedoodledoo!"

"You are indeed a venerable ruin," declared Martin, sighing gently. "What about the other two times?"

"The second time was a straightforward side kick straight into my rib cage during a sparring competition. The other chap was much quicker than me but I was over confident anyway. In the previous bout I had caught someone fair and square on his nose and he had a big bleed too. The awful thing about it, Martin, is that I felt a huge elation at hitting this perfect stranger so well! I have a bit of an aggressive side which I hadn't realised before. Anyway, I carried on this next bout okay 'til the end, though I lost it easily. The ribs were sore but not too bad until the next weekend. A friend of mine had persuaded me to do a seven-mile running race that weekend. I love running but mainly for the solitude. God knows why I had agreed to join this run. Anyway, I was pottering along in the middle of a pack of two or three hundred people when wham! Agony shot through my chest. It was exactly where I had been kicked and it hurt so much, I just couldn't breathe. You can imagine that the rest of that run wasn't fun. I could just make the end with one arm clutching my chest wall but boy, was I glad to finish! I must have cracked a rib when I was kicked and it went completely as I was puffing around the run. It all settled okay though."

"And the third time?" enquired Martin, with a resigned look on his face.

"The third injury happened when I was actually doing the Black Belt test."

"Black belt!" exclaimed Martin "You're a bloody dark horse, Bill!"

"Not at all," Bill responded, "I failed it anyway. Three of us hopefuls had travelled all the way up to Doncaster where there was a black belt grading set up for people from all over the country. I got a smack in the mouth during the sparring part of the test and apart from blood all down my tunic and a loosened front tooth, I lost marks for not keeping my guard up. I did just about everything else wrong as well, except for breaking a board with a side kick, which in practice was the only thing I could never do. Actually, once I broke that board, I thought I may have passed. The results were posted to you about a week later. I had about a week thinking I may have passed before the results letter put me right. I decided to settle for that. I had done five years of it by that time and was about to go and work in Australia, so that was the end of my time in Tae Kwando."

"A life blighted by failure then," said Martin, smiling as he spoke.

"It has given me a sort of confidence. Some of the men I met were very impressive. One of them told me that if someone threw a glass of beer in his face and whacked him with a punch, he would walk away rather than degrade himself in a pub brawl. And he was someone who appeared fearless and was certainly very formidable. You only saw it in the competitions. I guess he had nothing to prove. The other thing I learned was that being hit quite hard, wasn't half as bad as it looks. I stopped being scared of being hit. The other thing about being scared is that the competitions were, to start with, overpoweringly scary for me. I lost one of my first ever bouts just by cowering in the corner. Hopeless! Afterwards I had time to reflect and realised that the chance of serious injury was negligible. From then on, I was able to give it all I had — which often wasn't much Martin but it was enough for me to keep my head up!"

"That's interesting Bill. Do you think it's worth me giving it a go then?"

"Absolutely yes." Bill had no doubts about his response. "You will feel old and slow compared to the others but you will learn from them and the instructors will modify things according to how you are making out. Everyone has to learn a series of patterns. They are groups of movements with kicks and punches which are associated with each belt grading you do. I still do the patterns from white belt to black belt as part of my morning exercise routine." Bill didn't tell Martin that all morning exercise routines were currently on hold due to his feelings of fatigue.

"The other really good thing about the whole show is the contact with young people. They are full of fun, energy and are incredibly friendly. For me, as a doctor at the time, it was great to meet healthy youngsters, as opposed to the poorly ones with glandular fever, or drug problems or eating disorders — which were my usual contact with youth. These kids make you feel alive yourself. Yes Martin, you have started and that's the difficult bit. Stick with it my friend, it will be worth it!"

Martin leaned forward across the bar and fetched Bill a rattling slap on his shoulder.

"Is that the sexually transmitted disease clinic?"

Bill knew that the current name for the clinic was the GUM clinic, which stood for Genito-Urinary Medicine but he just hadn't warmed to the term.

"Yes, can I help you?"

"Oh good. Well, I am actually feeling well but have a new, er, sexual partner," ('am I actually saying this? he thought to himself') "and we have agreed to get ourselves checked out, as it were."

"That's fine," returned a reassuringly matter of fact voice "If you haven't got any symptoms, we can do most of it from a urine sample. Do you want to have an HIV test as well?"

"Yes, indeed."

"Okay. We will need to see you for a pre-test talk and then get a sample of blood from you"

"Excellent"

"Your name then please"

"William Smith"

There was a discernible pause before,

"You are not Doctor William Smith, by any chance, are you?"

"Yes, that's me."

"Well hello Bill! I thought your voice sounded familiar. How nice to hear from you. The last I heard you were out in Africa."

Bill had been hoping to slide through the system incognito. He had at one time worked in the clinic doing a couple of sessions a week but that had ended a good twelve years ago.

"You've got a better memory than me," he said, "you sound familiar but I can't put a name to your voice."

"It's Angela. I'm still on reception just the same as in your day. Mind you, things have changed a lot since you were here. You needn't worry about anyone sliding a cotton bud up you now, doctor, not for your sort of check anyway. That's a bit of luck, isn't it? Now then, when would you like to come?"

"I can fit in with you. I'm retired now."

"Well Doctor, if you like, there happens to be a gap in two hours' time. Can you make that?"

Bill hesitated. His car was being serviced and the hospital housing the clinic was fourteen miles away. Completely forgetting his new 'take it easy' approach to life, he made the decision.

"Yes, I will be there."

"We shall look forward to seeing you very soon, Doctor."

Bill wandered into his kitchen and drank a glass of water. He tucked his chinos into his socks, strode into the small outhouse beside his home and took out his bike.

The main road which connected Tregannion to the main hospital in Truro was a busy affair but Bill knew the backroads well, and worked his way through a labyrinth of narrow, hedge-lined country lanes. As he cycled along, he mused over the casual enquiry about the HIV test. Few people alive had seen the ravages of the disease more vividly than Bill. For him, it was a staining mark which had soaked through his first visit to work in a small government hospital in South Africa. That was back in 1996, when the official and local view of HIV and AIDS was of denial. Sometimes as many as twelve young people died in a single day from the disease in the hospital. Their bodies were thin and emaciated but their faces remained youthful and they didn't want to die. On their death certificates went conditions such as tuberculosis, gastro-enteritis or meningitis. The underlying cause which had enabled these infections to take their lethal hold remained unwritten. The truth was carefully ignored.

'Just give me something to improve my appetite' was the standard request. Bill not only felt impotent, in the face of such a plague but was immensely frustrated when the nurses refused to even discuss the subject, saying, 'It's a private matter' as the end-of-life care of the dying was being worked out.

Things got better. Bill made three visits to the hospital over three years, each visit lasting three months. On the second visit, the nurses had dramatically changed their attitude. Such was the death rate that the hospital school of nursing attempted each year to enrol twice the number of students as would be required on the wards, in their effort to counter the inevitable reduction in numbers due to the ambient death rate. Now there was an active discussion going on about the disease and an active interest had replaced the distressing mood of wilfully blind silence.

On Bill's final visit, not only was the disease openly talked about but a new doctor had been assigned to offer treatment with anti-retroviral drugs. He was having some success and a corner had been turned.

Bill himself had been involved in a variety of surgical procedures, including caesarean sections and was aware that a needle stick injury, or a nick from his own scalpel blade could easily have allowed the virus to invade his own body. The estimate at the time was that forty per cent of the mothers beneath his knife were HIV positive. As far as he remembered, no such incidents had occurred to him and on return to the UK, a check HIV test had been clear. He was grateful for the chance of a double check now, though the stakes were far too high for a slip up of that magnitude.

The GUM clinic was superb in friendliness and efficiency. Four days later, Bill received a text telling him that he was all clear.

Amelia wanted to arrange a time for their first rendezvous, which she was describing as their get-together. It soon became obvious to Bill that hers was a different approach to the usual romance-based liaisons he had previously engaged in. Firstly, Amelia's diary was remarkably full. Alan was due to leave shortly but his departure was immediately followed by a visit from one of Amelia's girlfriends. The first likely date appeared to be about three weeks away but the sudden recollection of her likely period week pushed things back to almost a month.

"Well never mind," she had said airily, "I love looking forward to things and it will give you plenty of time to work out your next talk for us all!"

Amelia wanted to explore the physical world of Tantra and Bill was the first person she had met who felt suitable. She couldn't define exactly what that was and she had some concerns about the idea. The natural inclination to follow her instinct had won the day but her concerns were for him as much as herself. He had a lonely look about him sometimes and might be emotionally more vulnerable than he appeared. She was finding that their age difference felt somewhat protective to her. He was hopefully less likely to fall madly in love with her, a state of mind which she would find irksome and a burden to carry around.

THE THIRD WOMEN'S INSTITUTE TALK

Bill did indeed put his mind to the task of his next talk, which was due in ten days' time. The WI talks held both a connection to Amelia and a much-needed distraction.

The next talk had to be peppery and to the point. He felt strongly about the issues. On the assigned evening he struck out to the WI hall, with a jaunty and almost festive air. Passing straight by the pub with the clear intention of calling in on his return walk, he reminded himself that this talk was important. He intended to disseminate truth and eradicate error. Dr William Vesuvius Smith was feeling enjoyably animated.

Shortly afterwards, standing at the same podium in front of the same ladies, Bill waited for the expectant hush to fall. Amelia, who had welcomed him in as usual, was seated at the back of the hall and it was with an effort of will he got his mind off her and on to the issue of the moment.

"Ladies." Bill always made a point of getting his very first word out loud and clear. It was not so much getting the audience to hear, as it was him getting used to the sound of his own voice ringing out, which boosted his confidence.

"The Saturday Times of August the 8th 2020 has a front page picture of four Africans paddling a small inflatable boat, using shovels as paddles, as they tried to cross the Channel from France to England. The picture made me feel quite emotional. I have worked in Africa and recognised the qualities of courage and improvisation that these young men were using. God knows what they had been through to even reach the French coast, let alone ours. Their stories are largely hidden from us but I am of the opinion that such people represent the bravest, the most resourceful and the most determined of their kind.

"I am not an Africa enthusiast. I worked there but unlike many of my European colleagues, Africa didn't entice me with its undoubted beauty and challenges. Some of my time was spent in South Africa, in KwaZulu-Natal. Initially, it was difficult to overcome prejudice against me because I was white in an all-black hospital. Apartheid has left a lasting scar. But when the black nurses realised I would come when they called me, and I really was working on their side, life became normalised. In Zambia, I was working in the South Luangwa Nature reserve. Beautiful yes but you couldn't go running in the woods because of wild elephants, you couldn't go swimming in the river because of the crocodiles and, in the evening, a glass of wine on the veranda became dangerous because that is when the mosquitoes get going. They inject little doses of malaria for free. England, I came to realise, had more advantages than I had realised!

"Nonetheless, I was successful in getting to know the people I was working with and treating. Believe me, they are exactly the same as us. They bleed like us, they feel pain like us, they laugh like us. They make love to each other the same as we do. They seek a decent life like we do. They require the same basics which should be the right of every human being.

By this I mean food, shelter, clothing and education, all underwritten by basic sanitation. Given decent conditions, a lively and healthy sense of fun emerges and these people show themselves to have the same mix of qualities as we Europeans do. We are the same.

"I will qualify that a little: generalising hugely of course, Europeans seem to be better than Africans at planning, maintenance and scheduling. Africans are better than we Europeans are at grabbing the moment. They can find laughter from a field of despair. If you want to be inspired by Africans, watch the children playing in a river. Their glistening bodies are both healthy and beautiful. Their laughter is infectious. If you want to see muscularity, balance and poise, watch an African woman carrying a pitcher of water, or a heavy bundle of firewood on her head. If you want to be spiritually lifted, listen to an African women's church choir singing on a Sunday.

"I believe that Europeans and Africans can each teach the other the same amount. Somewhere there is a middle ground that we would all do well to seek.

"Because of poor government, warfare, corruption and disease, some strike out for Europe, looking for a better life. From a European perspective, we slowly become aware of illegal immigrants desperately trying to reach our shores. What are we to do about it? I hear our government talking about curbing the problem but doing absolutely nothing about solving it.

"In a similar vein, on social media recently was the story of a Syrian Doctor. His home was bombed and he found himself looking at the bodies of his wife and his two older children. One child survived, a baby girl. The Doctor carried his daughter on foot over many miles. They managed to get into Europe after a dangerous sea passage. They made it all the way to the French coast. The passage across the Channel in an over-crowded dinghy was a trip too many for the baby girl. As water poured in, she succumbed to hypothermia. Her father was rescued and he now resides here in England seeking asylum.

"Can any of us here imagine anything worse? His tale of woe is hidden. The Doctor becomes just another illegal immigrant and yet another problem to solve. Ladies, I want to suggest that something better could be done for such people. For the sake of this talk, I will talk about Syrian refugees only, though the same principles could be applied to illegal African immigrants as well. Remember that currently, there are no solutions being voiced by our government, only a desire to curb. Sometimes it falls to us, the public, to initiate change."

Bill stopped to take a sip of water. His glance around the room was reassuring, as attention seemed total.

"The Syrian conflict is one where people seem determined to fight each other. Most of us will never understand the issues, although probably there is an underlying animosity between the Sunni and Shia religious groups which goes back centuries. It might be comparable to previous schisms between Catholic and Protestant groups within the Christian world.

"Now, who wants to join in such a battle when from our perspective it isn't easy to pick out the good guys? The bad guys might suddenly appear not quite so bad after all, there are groups who seem a bit in between and, suddenly, more groups crop up who are so bad that it might be worth joining up with the original bad guys after all.

"It is too complicated for outsiders to understand. By contrast, what is very easy to understand is the effect of the fighting. Imagine your city being reduced to rubble, your home destroyed. Imagine the horror of injuries and the death of loved ones.

"So ladies, what I propose is this, it is very simple. Throughout the UK, every village, town and city be asked how many Syrian refugees they would like to house and support. Some answers will be a simple zero and whatever the reason, this must be respected. Where there is a positive response, that number of refugees should be guided there, to places where they have been welcomed

"This is not the same as opening doors to unlimited numbers of refugees. To do that will induce unrest and right-wing reactions will be aggressive. They will use the introduction of refugees into our country as an excuse for violence and disorder. We must ensure that every refugee admitted has a welcome and a home to go to. Every individual, every community must have their say.

"Now then, the big question is what do we do with the unwanted refugees? The answer is, we take them back. Not to the fighting zones but to decent refugee camps either close to Syria, or in peaceful but defendable areas within Syria itself. We will help construct these camps. Today, on the TV, we see pictures of tent cities, ill-equipped to face an ordinary winter. We can do better than that. We will construct not only homes but schools, hospitals and all the essential services that are needed to give people a decent life. Then, ladies, most importantly, we will defend such camps. We can give our armed forces a noble cause, a cause that rises above the calamity of warfare. They will be protecting our love in action and they will not only be able to feel proud of what they do, but they will inspire others to join them."

"Dr Smith," came a voice from the audience "Are you saying that our soldiers should risk their lives in this foreign war?"

Bill recognised the voice of Mrs Caldicott straight away. She was a near neighbour of his and well-known for her strong opinions.

"Yes, I am. The armed forces are for fighting and that means risking lives. You can't send a bunch of boy scouts. They need to be properly equipped, professional soldiers. Mind you, they would never get mixed up in the fighting of the war. Their job is to protect the refugee camps, nothing more but nothing less either."

"I don't want our soldiers being killed in a foreign war."

"Well," replied Bill, "such a task would be a far more noble cause than fighting in a war which we don't fully understand. That, I agree with you, would be insane. Think though, how the good will from this approach would last for generations, both with the help we could offer here in the UK, as well as in the refugee camps themselves."

"Who would pay for it?" came another question from the gloom.

"It would cost a lot less than going to war in Iraq, don't you think? We must remember that Syrians are not only skilled and productive people but when the fighting stops, many of them will be wanting to get home again as soon as possible. With them, they will take their impressions of us, the British people. What we do or don't do now will leave an impression on generations yet to be born."

"Supposing the Russians bomb us." It was Mrs Caldicott again.

"That would be unlikely, considering that it will be made

crystal clear that we have no engagement in the actual war. The adverse publicity from such an attack would be huge. No one could say for sure what would actually happen. The question is, Mrs Caldicott, do you think we should do anything at all, or are you happy to let them get on with it and block anyone we can from getting across the Channel?"

Mrs Caldicott remained quiet but another question came and Bill felt pleased that there was a response. Some of them had been listening!

"Wouldn't it all cost too much, Doctor? After all, we are talking about millions of people, not just a few thousand. I am not exactly disagreeing with your idea but I don't think you are being realistic."

"Yes, you are right. Our country alone cannot manage the whole problem. We can, however, show the rest of the world a simple system which could fix things. Right now, Turkey is harbouring huge numbers of refugees. The conditions are so bad that decent, ordinary people are risking all to escape. Greece is sitting next to Turkey and is getting inundated. What do you think yourselves? Is it just their problem? Is it OUR problem? Surely it is EVERYONE'S problem. Do we really want to help? Supposing we agreed on the number of people who could be genuinely welcomed here and then provided properly for a small group of the rest in decent and safe refugee camps, then we can shout out loud to the rest of the world, 'Come on! Where are you America, France, Germany, China, Brazil?' Our country has a great chance to lead from the front. I mean lead. Leadership is what is lacking. Right now, I feel that putting up a Channel blockade is an affront to humanity. We can do better! Think of the bereaved Syrian Doctor. Is there one amongst us who wouldn't offer help if we could? The help needs to be organised. Our government needs to hear from us, ordinary people, what we want it to do!"

Bill had been steadily raising his voice. He became aware of what he was doing and it prompted him to a much-needed slowing of tempo and volume.

"Ladies," he continued more sedately, "remember as before, to ask yourselves, is what we are doing working for us, the refugees themselves, for mankind in general? If you feel the Channel blockade is the right answer, then rest content. If you think it is not working, then ask yourself what would work and start thinking, talking and finally acting on your idea."

Bill glanced around. They didn't look bored but he knew he should finish fairly quickly now. He started again, gently and quietly.

"President Obama strikes me as being a good man. He is thoughtful, articulate and as far as I can make out, he means well. However, in his last six months in office, he was completely eclipsed by Donald Trump, who wasn't even in power and by Vladimir Putin who had decided to sway the war in Syria his way, with vicious bombing raids. Had President Obama initiated a plan like the one I have put before you tonight, the world would be a better place than it is today and President Obama would have rightly made his mark on the world. He didn't act.

"It is not enough just to be good.

"Ladies, once again, Thank you for your time."

Amelia led the applause. As Bill made his usual passage through the room towards the exit, she leaned towards him as he passed.

"Are you calling in at the Red Lion, Doctor?"

"Yes," replied Bill. "I'm going to stir up Martin a little."

"Good. I am giving several people here a lift home after the meeting but will pop in to see you there. There has been a slight change of plan which helps us a little. See you soon."

She smiled a goodbye and Bill made his way out, feeling as merry as a wedding bell.

At the pub, Martin was busy for the first half an hour after Bill had secured his usual corner seat. Looking around, he was quite impressed at the obvious compliance that most people were displaying to the social distancing rules. It was Bill's feeling that people were generally nice creatures and allowances should be made for the occasional mistakes and slip-ups that trip everyone up at some stage or other. He didn't want to fraternise and remained content, people watching. A large lantern-jawed man sat a couple of yards away from Bill. He was gazing motionlessly down at his glass of beer, as though mentally contemplating some sublime relic of bygone grandeur. Perhaps not though. Often people like that were not thinking of anything at all. Their minds were switched off, empty.

Bill heard Martin offering insults to one of his regulars at the other end of the bar.

"Get out of here you snivelling blaggard!" was the insult he was throwing at a serious-looking, elderly man who was clearly used to such verbal assaults from his landlord. It marked the end of their conversation, as Martin was strolling along the bar towards Bill. He was looking in good form, Bill observed, as he approached. There was a slight swagger in his gait and his clothes looked noticeably dapper. His shirt was of a cowboy red and brown checked pattern. The trousers, still tight about the waist, were white cords.

"Hello Bill," he said "You are a comfort to the eye. That old geezer has been trying to persuade me that we have made a calamitous decision over Brexit. I told him straight that he was uttering nothing but a murky blasphemy. He doesn't know what democracy is, when he's on the losing side. I told him that now is our chance to get the country right. And what's more, Boris Johnson is a Prime Minister who actually does what he says. Winston Churchill himself would be proud of him."

Bill, who had felt an instinctive fearfulness over the Brexit decision himself, merely smiled at the slightly riled-up friend of his over the bar. A gratis pint of beer was already pouring into a glass for him. Martin went on.

"I'm going to Tae Kwando twice a week now, Bill. I'm feeling better about myself already and a wee bit fitter. You were right to nudge me as I wasn't sure about it. I've got the bug now though! Anyway, what's the best with you then, my old mate? Are you still boring those long-suffering WI women? What did you depress them with this time?"

"Oh, we talked about refugees," said Bill simply.

"Illegal immigrants you mean. They should be sent back straight away," declared Martin somewhat predictably. "There's no space for them here. If they cock it up in their own countries, why should we bail them out here? Bloody ridiculous."

"Pity you missed the talk, really," replied Bill. He knew of Martin's opinions from old and had no desire to argue with him. He studied him a bit more closely. His hair was thick and for a man Bill guessed of being about forty years of age, was still a healthy brown colour, with no evidence of artificial colouring. He had an occasional habit of pawing at his hair when over-busy, when his usual neat coiffure became rumpled. Further conversation ended abruptly as Bill suddenly became aware of Amelia striding through the bar towards him.

"Hello Bill," she said warmly. "Great talk. I've left them all discussing the rights and wrongs of it. Several ladies had seen the picture in The Times you mentioned. Anyway, I can't stay now. I am giving three ladies a lift home, so have just popped in to say that the meeting I was going to tomorrow has been cancelled. We are doing it in the evening by Zoom instead. That means I am free tomorrow, so if you happen to be free too, we can have our get-together tomorrow."

"Yes," said Bill, his heart missing a beat. "I can come around tomorrow."

"Brilliant," she declared. "Will ten o'clock suit you?"

"I will see you then."

Amelia left, dropping the briefest of kisses on his cheek as she did so. Her compliance to social distancing was scant, Bill observed, at least in regard to him.

The die had been cast.

"What's that all about then Bill?" asked Martin, who had politely turned away as Amelia had approached.

"Oh, nothing much. We meet up occasionally to sort out the next talk I am going to give. And you, Martin, have given me the idea for the next one. I will talk about Brexit and I might just investigate what Winston Churchill would have thought about what our mighty Boris is up to, while I am at it."

"You'll wake up a nest of bloody hornets if you talk about Brexit, that's for sure," Martin replied. He shuddered briefly and scowling fearfully repeated,

"A nest of bloody hornets!"

CATCH UP WITH AMELIA

Bill was punctual in his arrival at Amelia's house. He had not slept well due to an enervating mixture of adrenaline and anticipation. Nonetheless, at some time in the night he had drifted off to sleep and had woken feeling refreshed. He had washed himself carefully. His genitals and under the foreskin were treated to a shampoo douche. He cut his fingernails neat and short. He avoided a prolonged inspection of himself in the mirror other than to neatly comb his bald head, before he pronounced himself nearly ready for the rendezvous. There was one thing left to do. He had considered the option of a tablet to aid erection and had decided to use one. The type he opted for was called Cialis. It was easily available from a doctor, or from the internet. Bill had used the Superdrug online purchasing method. He had used it before and knew it worked brilliantly on him. He also knew that his erections were frequent and spontaneous, so he had no anxiety about his bodily function. What he was aware of though, was that sometimes the adrenaline of a new sexual journey could slow down his erectile response. His partner, who might also be feeling nervous, could misinterpret his slowness as a sign that she was not attractive to him, resulting in a downward spiral of desire and function. The tablet strength Bill had was 20mg. Using a sharp knife, he cut one in half and swallowed an approximate 10mg. The effect should last for thirty-six hours and previous experience had shown that to be the case. Bill felt good. He was presentable, alert and ready to rise to the occasion.

He walked to Amelia's home, a pleasant stroll which took him nearly thirty minutes. Although Tregannion was twelve miles from the sea, he was sure he could sniff saltiness in the air. He was pleased to reach the turning which took him into the lanes outside of the village. Autumn was just beginning to show itself and although the hedgerows were still green to the casual glance, the tarmac between was speckled with brown- and orange-coloured leaves, the early seasonal droppings from surrounding tree life. He was in just the right mood. The gentle exertion of his walking was balancing the ride of adrenaline he was walking with. The air had a moist feel, it was cooling, calming, perfect. He straightened his posture, pulled his slim belly inwards and standing tall he marched along with every outward appearance of a young man on the move.

Amelia opened the door smiling and enveloped him in a tender hug. He smelt her hair and felt the soft pressure of her body, causing an immediate physical response. He hoped he hadn't overdone the Cialis.

"Let's have a cup of tea to start with Bill. I am so thrilled you are here. Sit in the lounge and I will be in in a few minutes. Now, you don't take sugar, do you?"

"No," said Bill, answering her rhetorical question. He sat down at one end of a long sofa and perused the room. Among the photographs dotted around was a strong-looking, young man in military uniform who he guessed was probably her deceased husband. There was another picture of a young-looking Amelia with the same man, both seated on a motor bike. Bill reflected briefly how little most people actually knew about each other. There were so many hidden stories behind every living soul. Other pictures showed two children at varying ages. They must be her son and daughter he surmised. His eyes scanned the lines of books filling several ranks of shelves. There was an impression of both organisation and chaos about the books, with sections of travel having a book on cooking stuffed in the middle and a section on languages being invaded by a book on mountaineering.

"Here we are." She came in and lowered a tray of tea cups, milk and a covered tea pot onto a low table, then sat at the other end of the sofa. Bill forgot about the room and gave her all his attention.

"Shall I be Mum?" he asked.

"Please go ahead," she replied. "It will be just about ready by now"

Their small talk had a nervous intimacy about it.

"Here you are, my dear," Bill leaned cross to pass her the tea.

"My dear," she repeated, "I like that," and she leaned across to rest her hand briefly on his. "You are a dear too you know. There's no one else in my world I could have asked to visit me like this."

"Well, here I am, and I know this is special for us both. Cheers to us then!" He raised his cup of tea in a gentle toast to them both and Amelia beamed at him.

They drank the tea in a pensive silence, neither feeling quite sure how to end the quietness. Their empty cups returned to their respective saucers in unison.

Amelia leaned across to Bill and took his hand.

"Come with me," she said.

She led him through the hallway, into the darker corridor on the opposite side and into the first room on the right. It was her downstairs bedroom, easily confirmed by the paraphernalia of womanhood on the dressing table and the casually made bed, revealing recent use.

With no more words passing between them, Amelia started slipping out of her clothing. After a few seconds, Bill followed suit and within a minute they faced each other, naked. Bill smiled at her and placed a hand on each of her shoulders and gently rotated her around, so she was now back to him. Very gently, he pulled her back on to himself feeling the pleasurable shock of her soft skin coming into contact with his own. He pressed his head against hers, relishing her scent and the soft feel of her hair. He slid his hand over her scalp and firmly gripping a handful of hair, turned her head towards him. He met her gaze, apprehensive but open and then he kissed her. Her lips were soft. They tensed against the pressure from his lips, then parted. Bill felt the tentative touch of her tongue, moist, exciting. He responded with a small touch of his own against hers and suddenly his mouth became invaded by a probing, thrusting and squirming tongue that thrilled him with its power, intrusiveness and unexpectedness. His mouth was still filled with her, when she swivelled around in his arms and he felt her breasts, her belly and thighs press against him, as her tongue probed deeper.

Slowly, she withdrew from him, panting a little. She looked up at him and he saw her hope, her need and her anticipation. With his hands holding her upper arms he manoeuvred her to the edge of the bed. Very quietly he said,

"Lay down."

Amelia laid back on the bed, smiling up at him. Bill slid

himself over the top of her, to lay on his side alongside her. He smiled back at her. Passing his upper arm over to her far shoulder, he pulled her towards him. He leaned forward and took her mouth again. This time the meeting of tongues was more equal, as their embrace reached an oral intimacy, which fired their desire for each other.

Bill felt Amelia's hands on his head; she was pushing him gently downwards.

"Kiss me again," she said softly, "here."

She directed Bill down and over the soft curve of her right breast. As he felt her softness against his cheek, she pressed him into her again. And then downwards. He sought her nipple, he licked it and then sucked the brownness and hardness of it deep into his mouth. A groan of pleasure rewarded him. He pressed her tissue between the roof of his mouth and his tongue, sucking hard every now and then, each suck causing a small moan to come from her. Her head was thrown back and her eyes, though open, were far away from his gaze. Her hands returned to his head, pushing him sideways.

"The other one," she whispered softly and urgently to him. He slid his mouth across her chest, already moist with tiny beads of sweat. He found the erotic softness of her left breast. He sought and found her nipple and sucked her harder this time. The groan was momentarily a shout of pain but immediately her hand returned to his head and pressed him hard against her bosom. He softened his action, relaxed himself and became aware that the feel and sight of her breasts against his face and inside his mouth was causing a pleasure that was steadily being enhanced by his own swelling below.

Amelia's hands, both hands, pushed down on the top of

his head. No words were spoken. The pressure guided him past her umbilicus, down over the soft curve of her belly and suddenly, he was touching the dark, curly hair of her pubes. Bill was aroused by the sight of her most private hair, the dark, almost black colour, the most intimate of feel and then, over riding all, the smell of her. The musk-like smell of a woman's vulva reaches a visceral level in male human sexual desire that goes back to creation. His nose sucked in the perfume from the Gods. He was filled with strong desire and helpless to its effect. He lifted his hands to the sacred part of his woman and parted her lips. Her legs were laying open for him and he glimpsed the startling pink of the hidden, secret place which lay so seductively behind the screen of erotic hair. Bill knew he was in a paradise on earth. His tongue passed forward on to her and he licked her most tender and sensitive spot, that now lay revealed to him. Her hands lay firm on either side of his head again, making small adjustments to his position. Soon he heard a tight whisper,

"A little harder."

Bill pressed his tongue against her, sweeping upwards time and time again, until he ached. He was rewarded by feeling little shudders pass through her. Looking up, he could see past the fringe of dark, pubic hair, past the swell of her belly and the fall of her breasts to her face which was upturned, her lips were parted, her breathing was deep.

Her thighs began to press against him, in time with the little shudders, which soon became less little and more frequent, with more sounds until a cry broke across the room and the soft muscularity of her thighs clamped together locking Bill into her hair, her smell, her softness, the essence of her femaleness.

It seemed a long time, Bill didn't know or care. He was in paradise himself. Slowly, the pressure eased from his ears and her thighs opened in their release of him. Again, he felt her hands. Amelia's hands were now urgently pulling him upwards over her moist body. He slid easily over her until their mouths were level. They kissed again. Amelia seemed thrilled by her own taste, which lingered strong in Bill's mouth. The kiss was long, deep and thrilling, when Amelia pushed back Bill's head and said quietly.

"Come into me"

Bill slid upwards another inch and immediately felt his hardness press into her softness. Amelia flicked her pelvis forward and Bill felt his penis pass between the slippery, guarding lips of her vagina. He was poised at her very introitus. He moved in a tiny bit. Amelia pulled at his hips to bring him fully in but he ignored her. Having rested a few seconds, he made another small inward movement and then another and another. The movements grew stronger and deeper until the last was met with the thrilling impact of the base of his penis against her pubic bone — a meeting which caused a cry of pleasure to emerge from them both.

They lay together, still panting a little. Then Bill made a little thrust and another and slowly started a rhythm of gentle and pleasurable movement. The bed had an iron bedhead with vertical running bars supporting the cross bar. Bill reached forward and pulling on the bars pulled himself upwards further causing his penis to squeeze harder against Amelia with every thrust. The effect on her was immediate. Every upward pull with his arms caused a pressure on Amelia which made her gasp. Bill was slightly elevated by his grip on the bars and looked down on this gorgeous creature beneath him, hardly believing what he was seeing. With every upward thrust he made, he saw her breasts swing upwards, then fall again. They were blotchy pink now and wet with sweat. Bill loved the sight of her breasts, swinging to his movements but his pleasure was suddenly magnified a thousand times when Amelia reached up to him and grabbed his nipples between finger and thumb of each hand and pulled. She pulled hard. Exquisite pain and pleasure shot through Bill. The pleasure from his nipples found a direct connection with his penis. He looked at himself being pulled out of shape by this beautiful woman and suddenly the explosion of pleasure took root and he knew his game was nearly over. As his tipping point came, Amelia herself suddenly stiffened and arched her back. Her cry was accompanied by a tightening of her vagina, as Bill succumbed to the irresistible climactic sensation which squeezed throughout his body.

They relaxed together, both wet bodies breathing in unison. Bill slid to one side of Amelia, leaving his left arm draped over her and his hand cupping her breast. He was aware enough to still be enthralled at the sensation of the soft, curving weight of her breast and the incredible fact that she was offering her body to him. He closed his eyes, allowing himself to wallow in the warmth of the moment.

Bill awoke to the sound of Amelia entering the bedroom. She was wearing an oriental patterned, silk dressing gown, very similar to his own. She was carrying a tray loaded with two mugs of tea, bourbon biscuits and sliced strawberries.

"Wake up, lazy bones," she said, as Bill's eyes flickered open.

He felt an amazement at how rapidly familiarity had developed. He mused that probably the secret lives of couples the world over were remarkably similar.

"I wasn't asleep, just resting," he protested

"Ha! What about the snoring then?"

"I don't snore."

"Bollocks Bill! You are a liar too. Maybe that's why I am attracted to you. You have a naughty side. Perhaps I like that."

"Ever heard of a pot calling the kettle black?"

She sat beside him and he rose and took the mug of tea gratefully. The tray she placed between them, as she slid into one side of the bed.

"I know why I am attracted to you Bill. It's not complicated. First and foremost, I just sort of fancy you. That's the mystery of life really. It's hard to work out why, unless someone is built like an Adonis, or has pots of money. Even those things don't count for much. No, it's some sort of chemistry between people that we can't control and whatever it is, I can feel it between us.

Bill took her hand and squeezed it.

"The other thing," she continued, "is just as important, well, to me it is anyway. Most men are possessive creatures. You offer them sex and they think they own you. I sometimes want to enjoy sex but not at the expense of the rest of me, if you see what I mean."

She smiled brightly at Bill. "And I have enjoyed sex today, Bill. Thank you so much."

Bill, who himself had just experienced a peak of sexual pleasure himself, merely smiled quietly back at her, before saying quietly,

"You are a wonderful woman Amelia and I thank you

too."

She carried on, becoming animated.

"When I described the impressions I had taken away from those Tantra weekends, you seemed to understand. It's not about ownership of someone, it's about sharing and respect. The single thing that I admired most over those weekends was the couple who went for a walk and had a cup of tea, because they preferred that to the option of sex. Anyway, we've got both today!"

"Don't worry about feeling possessed or owned by me Amelia. For a start, I am probably twenty years older than you. That makes me incredibly grateful to share sex with you anyway. In truth, I am lucky enough to always feel an attraction to women of my own age and always have done. It's easier than lusting after young women full of youthful beauty, who look at you blankly if you mention the Beatles, or the Falklands war. But anyway, you have your own path to tread, Amelia. I don't know what it is but I'm damned certain it will be an exciting one. I want to be your supporter, not an old timer holding you back. That would be my worst nightmare."

"You are a darling," she murmured back. "I knew you would understand. Anyway, I sensed that about you and it's important to me. It might be important to you too."

"Of course it is. Life has a flow. Let's enjoy the energy and grab moments like this while they exist."

The subject was ended. Amelia had relaxed on hearing him and after a few companionable moments enjoying the strawberries and biscuits, she opened up the conversation again.

"You said you were doing one more WI talk didn't you? Am I right in the ghastly memory that it is going to be about

Brexit?"

Bill stretched, feeling his body getting back into gear.

"Yes indeed. I know the die has been cast now but there are a few aspects which I think might be interesting to your members. You said they were talking amongst themselves about the issues I have brought up before."

"God, yes!" Amelia snorted into her tea. "You are a stirrer, you know. A bloody mischief maker! No wonder I invited you into my bed!"

She dropped her mug, rolled over and caressed him. Her dressing gown fell open enough to allow one of her breasts to rest directly on Bill's chest. He felt an immediate response as an erection grew rapidly. He recognised the effect of the Cialis still at work. Even Amelia was surprised as his upright member slid upwards over her lower tummy.

"My God, you are a soldier Bill, look at you!"

Bill laughed.

"It's not exactly me Amelia. It's me and an aide d'erection in the form of half a tablet I took before coming here this morning. There wasn't really a need for it as it turns out, but in the past, I have been slow to get an erection up and once the lovely lady I was with thought that she wasn't attractive and everything spiralled downhill from there."

Amelia pressed her breast more firmly on to his chest and wrapped her fingers around his penis, giving playful squeezes.

"Okay my man but next time don't take anything, just bring the tablets with you. Nothing would give me more pleasure than playing with this little fellow here for as long as it takes and then I'll pop him inside me to keep him warm. Is that okay with you?"

'What a question,' Bill thought to himself briefly.

"If he doesn't want to play, then you will have the tablet on you anyway."

Having said that, Amelia mounted Bill and sank his penis deep inside her.

It was lunchtime when they emerged from the bedroom, both feeling elated at the hidden sides of each other they had just revealed to themselves.

"I have to be out by two," said Amelia. "I can do soup and a sandwich if you like."

"That would be lovely"

"Good. And it will give me a chance to hear the gist of what you want to say about Brexit. I can see you like prodding people to think more but surely this old potato is so dusted off, people will just groan."

"They probably will groan. Anyway, I'll let you do the soup and then I'll tell you why I think it's worth going over. I know the big decision has been taken but the reality of what it all means is up for grabs right now."

With a bowl of tomato soup on his lap and a plate of corned beef sandwiches beside him, Bill began his explanation.

"Decent, hardworking people throughout the country were fed up with the way things were going. An ex-military paramedic friend of mine, who I respect a lot, said to me, the country is going to the wall. The police are in a mess, so is the NHS, the teachers and the military. We've got to make a change. Well, I agree with that all right but most of the problems we are struggling with are home grown. We are blaming Europe when the benefits from being European outweigh the disadvantages. I think somewhere in the mindset of the British, is a feeling that once we were great, and on our own, we can be great again. Boris is being compared to Winston Churchill. Some people think that we won the war, so why are we subservient to Europeans now?"

"Well, we did win the war, didn't we?"

"We stood up to Hitler and are quite rightly proud of that. The Luftwaffe met its first determined resistance in the RAF and we can be proud of that too. We should be proud of all our military efforts but we didn't win the war and never could have. The German army was crushed by the Americans in the West, with our help of course and by the Russians in the East. Did you know how many Russians were killed in the war for every Brit?"

"Tell me."

"Fifty."

"Bloody hell. Perhaps that's why Putin was so dismissive of the D-Day memorial commemoration."

"You bet. The Russians will have their own version of history anyway. Mind you, they did express approval of the Brexit Leave vote!"

"Well, what has all this got to do with where we are now? The war is really ancient history to most people."

"The war is relevant still. After it ended, Churchill was the instigator of the coming together of European countries. He wanted the structure of Europe to change so that we all got to trade and get to know each other and fighting would become unthinkable."

"What did he do?"

"He made a famous speech about it in Zurich after the war. I need to look up the details yet but I would regard him as the founding father of the European Union. God knows what he would say to Boris and his henchmen, who are actually being compared to him."

"Okay, two ticks, I'll check it out on Google."

Amelia disappeared briefly to reappear with her iPad. Her fingers ran rapidly over its surface.

"Now then, Winston Churchill, post war, Europe," she murmured. "Okay, here it is. Oh, shit, Bill, there's a load here. Are you in a hurry? Let me read this out."

Bill nodded his agreement and settled more comfortably into his chair. "What are you reading from?" he asked.

"It's something by the European Commission. It's actually only a page long. Ready?"

"Fire away."

"Okay then. Winston Churchill, 1874–1965.

"Sir Winston Churchill was one of the first to call for the creation of a 'United States of Europe'. Following the Second World War, he was convinced that only a united Europe could guarantee peace. His aim was to eliminate the European ills of nationalism and war mongering once and for all.

"He formulated his conclusions drawn from the lessons of history in his famous 'Speech to the academic youth', held at the University of Zurich in 1946.

"'There is a remedy which in a few years make all Europe… free and… happy.

"'It is to re-create the European family, or as much of it as we can, and to provide it with a structure under which it can dwell in peace, in safety, and in freedom. We must build a kind of United States of Europe.'

"With this plea for a United States of Europe, Churchill was one of the first to advocate European integration to prevent the atrocities of two world wars from ever happening again, calling for a Council of Europe as the first step. In 1948, in the Hague, eight hundred delegates from all over Europe met, with Churchill as honorary president, at a grand Congress of Europe.

"This led to the creation of the Council of Europe on the 5th May 1949, the first meeting of which was attended by Churchill himself. His call to action can be seen as propelling a further integration as later agreed upon during the Messina Conference in 1955, which led to the Treaty of Rome two years later. It was also Churchill who would first moot the idea of a European army, designed to protect the continent and provide European diplomacy with some muscle. Furthermore, the European Court of Human Rights was created in 1959 — a decade after Churchill first championed the idea.

"Providing the inspiration to the people of Europe as the building factor in the allied fight against Nazism and fascism, Winston Churchill consequently became a driving force behind European integration and an active fighter for its cause."

Amelia paused as she finished the piece, before commenting in her own special way.

"Well fuck me! He wouldn't be too happy about Boris then!"

"No, he wouldn't," replied Bill, who was, as always, smiling at Amelia's choice of words.

He went on. "The puzzle to me is that they say history repeats itself but it seems that the older generation who were born closer to the war, voted to leave and the younger ones voted remain."

Amelia pondered this a moment and then said,

"Maybe the young ones were more aware of their loss of

freedom to travel within Europe than the older ones were. You're right though, it is strange. Mind you, there are about two million British people living in Europe at the moment. They would have all have voted remain. They may well have been older. I wonder how many of them actually voted."

"I think it's because people here are blaming Europe for our problems, when the real problem is here with us all the time. We need to be sorting ourselves out."

"Well," returned Amelia, "isn't this old hat, like I said? Who wants to go over this again?"

"Well, I want to highlight Churchill's opinions at the time and his role in setting up the European Council. Personally, I think the risk to peace is the biggest risk of us leaving Europe. Just as it is facing real strains, we are spearheading the collapse. We have such an opportunity to strengthen, not weaken."

"HAD," replied Amelia, "the vote is done and dusted and you seem to keep forgetting that."

"I've not forgotten at all," he protested. "But you and I have known nothing but peace. It's easy to take it for granted. Now as we are negotiating, are our representatives thinking of European integrity at all? My impression is that all they want is the best financial deal for us that they can wring out of the Europeans. There isn't even a thought about looking after the interests of the other side. It's all manoeuvres and stealth tactics, when it should be about collaboration and openness. We need people who understand the concept of WIN-WIN. They need to seek agreements that benefit everybody. That's what Churchill was after, of course."

"Well Bill, good luck, that's all I can say. You generally cause a stir and I'm sure you will again. I'm sorry but I have to go soon. And oh, thank you for this morning. That was far more interesting than politics! Before we go though, get your diary out and let's sort out a date for our next get-together."

Amelia's diary was a busy one. They fixed their rendezvous at the first free spot, nearly three weeks away.

Bill left the house and walked towards his home, deciding quite quickly that a detour via the Red Lion was in order. Stillness reigned, the weather being balmy and delicious. There was just breeze sufficient to dance the leaves. Had he just experienced a singular sexual dream? No, his memory confirmed it, what had happened, had happened.

He dragged his mind around to their discussion. He wondered if he could find a copy of the whole speech that Sir Winston Churchill had delivered in Zurich back in 1946. He would have a go at finding it, in the meanwhile he could sound a few ideas out on Martin. He was a good testing point for any of Bill's thoughts. The contrary view was guaranteed to be stinging through his ears within seconds.

Bill entered the Red Lion and spotted that his usual seating point was empty. He made his way across and from his vantage point, could see Martin in conversation with a sumptuously-outfitted, middle-aged lady. She laughed frequently with a cheery screech and Bill could see that it was an escape for Martin to leave her and pass along the bar towards him.

"You are a comfort to the eye," he declared, resting an elbow on the bar. "How are you, my friend? Just lean across the bar a moment. I want you to see what I've got!"

Martin pointed under the bar and as Bill stretched over, he could just make out the shape of a large, black-coloured dog, its head resting quietly on its front paws. Querying brown eyes looked back at him.

"Got her yesterday," said Martin. "Took her over from my nephew who has had to change jobs. She's a retriever. Now if you ever need some exercise, just let me know. She loves running and I won't be doing enough with her. I have started mind. But she's yours for a run whenever you want her. She's called Maisie."

Bill could see that Martin was looking still trimmer. His complexion had become less ruddy, his belt less indenting.

"I will remember that, thanks Martin. I love running with dogs. I'm not running just at the moment, I'm giving myself a break but hope to get back to it soon. You're not looking bad yourself these days. Some running and Tae Kwando is sorting you out. Now then, my friend, after you've fetched me the usual Doom Bar, I want your opinion on something."

"You want my opinion on something! My fame is for lunacy Bill, so don't take notice of what I say."

"You think about stuff and have opinions. I know that you and I generally see the world from opposite ends but I like to know what your take is on things."

Martin strolled away to pull the beer, shaking his head as he did so.

"Has age laid its hand upon you at last, Bill, you crazy man? I bet you don't want to talk about sensible things like rugby, or cricket."

"No, I want to know how you feel about the role of the Prime Minister here in the UK."

"Oh, Jesus Christ, Bill! What on earth are you asking exactly?"

"Well, I feel that our Prime Minister should have an

elevated position, that puts them above party squabbles. Then they would have more time to contemplate big issues without party issues clouding their judgement. I would like them to have more contemplative time. They should expect morning coffee, afternoon tea and finish by 6pm. They need time to play with their family and early nights. Then we could expect sounder and better thought-out policies."

"Well how on earth are you going to separate the Prime Minister from the party that got him there?"

"Oh, that's easy," replied Bill, rapidly warming to the subject.

"After an election, every MP will vote on who they want to be the next PM. Now, this generally will be the leader of the largest elected party, as it is now. Sometimes though, the combined opposition groups will get a different person there. The differences to how things are now Martin are that, firstly, every MP will have an input, which sounds fair to me and, secondly, if the winner is the leader of a party, they will be relieved of that responsibility and the party itself will just vote in a successor."

"Oh, very clever," said Martin in a tone of patronising boredom. "There's not a snowball's chance in hell of getting a change like that through and you know it. Who would choose the cabinet anyway?"

"The new PM of course. But he could choose members from any party, not just his own. It would balance out power much better. And remember this."

Bill was aware of himself being in danger of becoming boring to Martin again.

"During the confusion over the Brexit votes, everybody said that Parliament wasn't fit for service. That's how I still feel but nothing has changed, absolutely nothing. So it's up to us to put a few ideas out there."

"Well, your idea sounds better, I agree. But you are a son of an air-filled beach ball, Bill. Stop wasting your time and energy on stuff you can't change. You're past twenty-one now old boy. You should be busy getting the garden in shape and then telling me all about your back ache."

"Piss off," replied Bill.

Their conversation was ended by the screeching lady at the other end of the bar, who had run out of her Sauvignon Blanc. Bill shuddered slightly. No one seemed to regard changing society as anything to do with them. Most seemed content just to throw insults at MPs. Bill knew that amongst those MPs were some well-meaning and highly motivated people.

"Well," he mused to himself, "even if they stuck to the same method of choosing a Prime Minister, surely they would be more measured, more statesman-like, if they were lifted out of their party problems and could look down on the whole picture."

Bill remembered his unease at Mrs Thatcher's ability to grind down opposition merely by having more night time stamina than them. He had thought back then that it would have been better if she took a good night's sleep. More recently, he and the rest of the country had witnessed Theresa May's exertions over Brexit. Even the Europeans felt sympathy for her, stuck fast as she was, slowly being crushed between the traditional rock and a hard place. Anyway, some ideas for his WI talk were coming to him.

He got home still wondering if he was just vainly seeking a mysterious and vanished glory of ancestors. No, he decided, he just wanted to express his ideas on improving how Parliament worked. It had often bemused him, that politicians, who exhibited obvious intelligence, would behave like squawking toddlers when attempting to settle an issue. Toddlers are firmly told to exhibit kindness and generosity to each other. They would be encouraged to share things and to think about others. Why do such qualities disappear from grown-up, super-intelligent politicians? Bill did agree with Martin on one point — he wasn't likely to change things. Still, he felt a lot better by getting things off his chest. The twenty or so ladies that were patiently listening to him at the WI were doing him the world of good. He was only going to give one more talk, so he would do his best to really stir them up.

On getting back home, his Google miracle know-all machine promptly threw up Sir Winston Churchill's speech about the United States of Europe in full. That, he decided, would be the start of his talk on Brexit which was due in a week's time. He wrote the speech down, word for word.

THE FOURTH WOMEN'S INSTITUTE TALK

Bill hadn't seen Amelia since their shared encounter together and it was already clear to him that she required nothing social from him, other than to sort out matters such as this talk. He remembered their diary date though and relished the thought.

"Good luck then," had been her last comments to him. "I hope the talk goes well. Don't be disappointed when they boo hoo you. Several of those ladies are all for Brexit."

Her smile was warm, her elbow greeting was emphatic and reassuring as he made his way into the hall. There before him sat the very same group of ladies. Bill was noticing that they seemed to sit in the same seats each time. He didn't normally bring written notes to read from when giving talks. This had rendered him a bit of a loose cannon on occasions when he had drifted mightily away from the subject. Today however, he carried the written-out speech that Sir Winston Churchill had delivered seventy-four years previously, before Bill had been born.

"Good evening, ladies," Bill began.

"I am going to recite you a few lines which will be familiar to you all. You will notice that the last line is changed. You may not like the change. I make the change to make a point. I will be talking about Brexit."

He cleared his throat and began,

"They shall not grow old as we that are left grow old.
Age shall not weary them, nor the years condemn
At the going down of the sun in the morning..."

"WE HAVE FORGOTTEN THEM."

There was an immediate rustling of discontent as he finished and Bill was not surprised when a hostile voice that had previously sprung from the centre of the hall, re-visited him with anger bristling through every syllable.

"Dr Smith, I have listened to your peculiar ideas out of a mixture of curiosity, amusement and pity. I will not, however, allow you to insult our glorious dead in this way. You should be ashamed of yourself! Our country is on the brink of finding itself again and it's a disgrace that people like you keep undermining everything that is being done. We have had two magnificent Prime Ministers in the past and we probably have one of equal calibre right now, in Boris Johnson. The other two are Sir Winston Churchill and Mrs Margaret Thatcher. All of them would abhor what you have just said. I am sorry, Dr Smith, this is just too bad!"

A thin ripple of applause followed her words.

Bill was unfazed. He had come to recognise in his doctoring, that anger can be reacted to entirely as he wanted. He didn't have to respond in kind, unless he wanted to. More often, a smile or an acknowledgement did the trick. Whichever he chose, he was in charge. On this occasion, he was inwardly thrilled at the three names she had thrown at him.

"I totally understand where you are coming from," he started.

"It is not the men and women who died that we have forgotten, it is the circumstances that led them into war in the first place. We will find common ground, rest assured, because what is clear to me is that we are both seeking the best for our country. This is a discussion about how best to achieve that."

He stopped and smiled at his audience, as some of them were unused to heated outbursts and were in need of reassurance.

"You mentioned Sir Winston Churchill. I am about to read out to you, word for word, a speech he delivered in Zurich back in 1946, before most of us were born. Before I do, I would like to reassure you that I too regard him as one of our all-time great Prime Ministers."

He quickly shuffled his papers. Reading out loud wasn't his forte. He preferred to wing it when talking publicly but this time there was no choice, so he set his mind to concentrate and get the job done well.

"This speech is entitled 'Speech to the Academic Youth' and these are Churchill's exact words:

"'I wish to speak about the tragedy of Europe, this noble continent, the home of all the great parent races of the western world, the foundation of Christian faith and ethics, the origin of most of the culture, arts, philosophy and science both of ancient and modern times. If Europe were once united in the sharing of its common inheritance there would be no limit to the happiness, prosperity and glory which its three hundred million or four hundred million people would enjoy. Yet it is from Europe, that has sprung that series of frightful nationalistic quarrels, originated by the Teutonic nations in their rise to power, which we have seen in this twentieth century and in our own lifetime, wreck the peace and mar the prospects of all mankind.

"'And what is the plight to which Europe has been reduced? Some of the smaller States have indeed made a good recovery but over wide areas a vast quivering mass of tormented, hungry, care worn and bewildered human beings, gape at the ruins of their cities and their homes and scan the dark horizons for the approach of some new peril, tyranny or terror. Among the victors there is a babel of voices; among the vanquished the sullen silence of despair. That is all that Europeans, grouped in so many ancient States and nations, that is all that the Germanic races have got by tearing each other to pieces and spreading havoc far and wide. Indeed, but for the fact that the great Republic across the Atlantic Ocean has at length, realised that the ruin or enslavement of Europe would involve their own fate as well and has stretched out hands of succour and of guidance but for that, the Dark Ages would have returned in all their cruelty and squalor. Gentlemen, they still may return.

"'Yet, all the while there is a remedy which, if it were generally and spontaneously adopted by the great majority of people in many lands, would as if by a miracle, transform the whole scene and would, in a few years, make all Europe or the greater part of it, as free and as happy as Switzerland is today. What is this sovereign remedy? It is to re-create the European Family, or as much of it as we can and to provide it with a structure under which it can dwell in peace, in safety and in freedom. We must build a kind of United States of Europe. In this way only will hundreds of millions of toilers be able to regain the simple joys and hopes which make life worth living. The process is simple. All that is needed is the resolve of hundreds of millions of men and women to do right, instead of wrong and to gain as their reward, blessing instead of cursing.

"'Much work Ladies and Gentlemen, has been done upon this task by the exertions of the Pan-European Union which owes so much to Count Coudenhove-Kalergi and which commanded the services of the famous French patriot and statesman Aristide Briand. There is also that immense body of doctrine and procedure which was brought into being amid high hopes after the first world war. I mean the League of Nations. The League of Nations did not fail because of its principles or conceptions. It failed because these principles were deserted by those States who had brought it into being. It failed because the governments of those days feared to face the facts and act, while time remained. This disaster must not be repeated. There is therefore much knowledge and material with which to build; and also bitter dear bought experience to stir the builders.

"'I was very glad to read in the newspapers two days ago that my friend President Truman had expressed his sympathy with this great design. There is no reason why a regional organisation of Europe should in any way conflict with the world organisation of the United Nations. On the contrary, I believe that the larger synthesis will only survive if it is founded upon coherent natural groupings. There is already a natural grouping in the Western hemisphere. We British have our own Commonwealth of Nations. These do not weaken, on the contrary they strengthen, the world organisation. They are, in fact, its main support. And why should there not be a

European group which could give a sense of enlarged patriotism and common citizenship to the distracted peoples of this turbulent and mighty continent? And why should it not take its rightful place with other great groupings and help to shape the onward destinies of men? In order that this should be accomplished, there must be an act of faith in which millions of families speaking many different languages must consciously take part.

"'We all know that the two world wars through which we have passed arose out of the vain passion of a newly united Germany to play the domineering part in the world. In this last struggle, crimes and massacres have been committed for which there is no parallel since the invasion of the Mongols in the fourteenth century and no equal at any time in human history. The guilty must be punished. Germany must be deprived of the power to rearm and make another aggressive war. But when all this has been done, then there must be an end to retribution. There must be what Mr Gladstone many years ago called 'a blessed act of oblivion'. We must all turn our backs on the horrors of the past. We must look to the future. We cannot afford to drag forward across the years that are to come, the hatreds and revenges which have sprung from the injuries of the past. If Europe is to be saved from infinite misery and indeed final doom, there must be this act of faith in the European family and this act of oblivion against all the crimes and follies of the past. Can the free peoples of Europe rise to the height of these resolves of the soul and of the instincts of the spirit of man? If they can, the wrongs and injuries which have been inflicted will have been washed away on all sides by the miseries that have been endured. Is there any need for further floods of agony? Is the only lesson of history to be that mankind is unreachable? Let there be justice, mercy, freedom. The peoples have only to will it and all will achieve their hearts' desire.

"I am now going to say something that will astonish you. The first step in the re-creation of the European family must be a partnership between France and Germany. In this way, only can France recover the moral and cultural leadership of Europe. There can be no revival without a spiritually-great France and a spiritually-great Germany. The structure of the United States of Europe, if well and truly built, will be such as to make the material strength of a single state less important. Small nations will count as much as large ones and gain their honour by their contribution to the common cause. The ancient States and principalities of Germany, freely joined together for mutual convenience in a federal system, might take their individual places among the United States of Europe. I shall not try to make a detailed programme for hundreds of millions of people who want to be happy and free, prosperous and safe, who wish to enjoy the four freedoms of which the great president Roosevelt spoke, and live in accordance with the principles embodied in the Atlantic Charter. If this is their wish, if this is the wish of the Europeans in so many lands, they have only to say so and means can be found and machinery erected, to carry that wish to full fruition.

"'But I must give you a warning. Time may be short. At present there is a breathing space. The cannons have ceased firing. The fighting has stopped; but the dangers have not stopped. If we are to form the United States of Europe, or whatever name it may take, we must begin now.

"'In these present days we dwell strangely and precariously under the shield and I will even say protection, of the atomic bomb. The atomic bomb is still only in the hands of a State and nation which we know will never use it except in the cause of right and freedom. But it may well be that in a few years, this awful agency of destruction will be widespread and the catastrophe following from its use by several warring nations will not only bring to an end all that we call civilisation but may possibly disintegrate the globe itself.

"'I must now sum up the propositions which are before you. Our constant aim must be to build and fortify the strength of the United Nations Organisation. Under and within that world concept, we must re-create the European Family in a regional structure called, it may be, the United States of Europe. And the first practical step would be to form a council of Europe. If at first all the States of Europe are not willing or able to join the Union, we must nevertheless proceed to assemble and combine those who will and those who can. The salvation of the common people of every race and of every land from war or servitude must be established on solid foundations and must be guarded by the readiness of all men and women to die, rather than submit to tyranny. In all this urgent work, France and Germany must take the lead together. Great Britain, the British Commonwealth of Nations, mighty America and I trust Soviet Russia — for then all the world would be, must be, the friends and sponsors of the new Europe and must champion its right to live and shine.

"Therefore, I say to you: LET EUROPE ARISE!"

Bill stopped and took breath. The audience remained silent.

"I am not able to deliver this speech to you with the largesse, the grandeur and the gravitas that would have accompanied its first delivery all those years ago," he said, "but the words are the same and to me, the message has lost none of its relevance. I am not asking you to think the same way as I do. I am asking you to think for yourselves, on this and every issue that comes our way."

"Doctor?" A new voice from the back floated through.

"Isn't this all too late? I mean, we have made the decision to leave Europe, so that's it isn't it?"

"Now is the moment of negotiating the terms of our future relationship. Our negotiators can be collaborative in approach, or stealthy, seeking only our benefit with no regard to the other side. 'No agreement' will be what some politicians are seeking anyway. Myself, I will always support a win-win agreement. If you come home with some kind of negotiating coup, while the other side is left diminished, it won't last. You haven't done yourself or your reputation any good. Win-win agreements are always there but they have to be actively sought. In this scenario, I fear that the agenda on our side is not to be open, not to be generous, in order to render the EU unable to make an agreement with us. Then our side will blame them for their intransigence. With no deal, or a weak deal, we just become a competitor to Europe on all trading matters, so Sir Winston's speech is still worth considering today."

The hostile voice came back

"I thought Sir Winston said that 'We are for Europe, but not of it'."

"He did," confirmed Bill. "Everything has to be taken in the context of the time, as far as we can. Churchill had some big disagreements with France's President Charles de Gaulle and he also was immensely grateful to the Americans for joining the war effort. He knew that President Roosevelt had been his and our saviour, so he had a strong affinity to

America. Since then, America and Europe have both moved on and perhaps we are lost in between. The Commonwealth has also changed enormously since that time. In the end, Churchill came down firmly in favour of joining the Common Market, as it was then."

"Doctor Smith," it was Mrs Caldicott, "I never felt we were influencing things when we were in Europe. Can you give me an example of where our influence, as just one of twenty-eight countries, could have been beneficial?"

"Indeed," replied Bill, again feeling gratitude for the question.

"Remember when I talked about the best response to the Syrian refugees? Angela Merkel opened the German borders to Syrians and huge numbers took advantage of a genuinely humanitarian response. However, they have had a predictable right wing, nationalistic backlash in Germany. Supposing we had whispered diplomatically, 'don't do that'. Ask first who wants to take in refugees and how many, as I described before. Then only manageable and welcome numbers are admitted. The whole of Europe could have then put money and muscle into providing decent living conditions for the rest. That could have come from us; it didn't. It could have come from America; it didn't. We could have not only demonstrated the idea ourselves but exhorted every European country to follow us. That is the sort of influence that we have currently lost. If the people of our country think for themselves, we can still get things right. But guidance from one of our best ever is in this speech."

Bill didn't add his personal fear that the current proposal to even discuss in Parliament a unilateral change to negotiated arrangements, which threatened to break international law, was melting away whatever influence on the world that still remained. He had deep personal forebodings, which he kept to himself.

The aggressive voice he had heard from the back before swung across at him again, a little less terse than before.

"Doctor. Don't you want to see our fishermen have the right to fish unhindered in our own waters?"

"I see it like this: if two toddlers are arguing over something they both want, they are rapidly exhorted to develop generosity, sharing and care for the other one. I don't know the ins and outs of the fishing regulations at the moment but I want our negotiators to behave like adults, seeking win-win solutions and not to behave like toddlers."

A silence fell over the hall and Bill was quick to call a break.

"We all need to stretch our legs, so let's all take ten minutes and we can then briefly return to another Prime Minister of the past, Mrs Margaret Thatcher."

As the room bustled with movement, Bill actively sought out Amelia who was, as usual, by the door at the back.

"Am I making a mess of this?" he asked earnestly.

She laughed in her encouraging way "So what if you are? It's great from my point of view. We will be mulling over your talks for ages. Anyway, just enjoy yourself. It's your last fling and you've got a captive audience, so make the best of it!"

Thus bolstered, he returned to the podium and gathered his thoughts for the final few words.

"Thank you, ladies. Now Mrs Thatcher has aroused huge support and also huge dislike. She was strongly pro-European with regard to the pan European trading opportunities for the UK, if not some other aspects. It is interesting to see now that areas which are benefitting most from European trade, in the car industry for example, are often the areas that voted to leave. We will come to that in a minute. First though, my own regard for Mrs Thatcher came because she brought power back to where it belongs, that is to the government. She came to power in the late 70s, when the workplace was in a chaotic state. Unions called regular strikes. We got used to postal strikes. There was shoulder-high garbage in London when the refuse collectors stopped work. Power worker strikes caused blackouts throughout the land and, of course, we had the divisive miner's strike. Abroad, we were known as the sick man of Europe. Well, Mrs Thatcher defeated the miners and whatever you think about the rights and wrongs of the issues, she certainly put the government back in the driving seat.

"As regards the UK needs for coal at the time, it was blandly assumed that we could just import it from Poland, America, Australia or Columbia, more cheaply than we could mine it for ourselves. Little thought was given to our self-reliance as a nation, nor the additional carbon footprint of transporting the coal around the globe, nor the human factors, such as the well documented use of child labour in Columbian mines.

"Many subsequent problems come from what the government has done since getting back into the driving seat.

"First came the de-regulation of the banks, which then allowed banks to lend large sums of money to house buyers. The rules of lending house buyers up to two and a half times their reliable annual income, carefully thought out with the local bank manager, disappeared, along with the bank managers. The result was an upward catapulting of house prices making homeowners feel smug and house buyers taking on ever increasing debt. An urgent rush to jump onto the ever-ascending housing ladder took grip. This became the underlying cause of the financial crash. Even a disinterested observer such as myself could forecast the crash several years before it happened, on the basis of seeing people borrowing more money than they could possibly hope to pay back. When the banks show such greed and arrogance, one looks to the government but nothing came to rein in behaviour and avert the crisis.

"Secondly, council housing was put on the market at bargain rates and many people naturally grabbed the opportunity.

"The result is what we have now — unaffordable housing for many and young families burdened by debt.

"An everyman for himself mentality grew in our society resulting in both winners and losers. Feelings of frustration were exacerbated in people like teachers, nurses and police — all seeing ludicrous salaries for footballers and bonuses for bankers in excess of their annual income.

"More recently, efforts to control the benefits scheme often seem to hit the poorest. This was at its worst during the austerity years, provoked by the banking crisis. So now we have been led into a time of food banks, homelessness and old people being afraid to turn on the heating in winter.

"A deep sense of grievance took root. When Mr Cameron said he wanted a referendum on membership of the European Union, as he tried to tidy up a divided Tory party, a visceral reaction to vote against him took root, which was not related to the issues that were on the table.

"We have voted ourselves out of a union that has provided us with a largely peaceful existence for over seventy years.

What would all the people who suffered and died in two world wars have given for the Europe we have all enjoyed? What would they be saying to us now?

"Well, the referendum certainly ended David Cameron's political career and the government now has the task of negotiating a trade deal which will inevitably displease many, whatever form it takes.

"We, the United Kingdom, never emotionally embraced the European vision. Prosperity came but we didn't share it fairly within our own country. Had we been visionary in the way Churchill was, he who saw the ravages of war, then we would have put our shoulder to the wheel to make the European dream a reality. No one is denying its faults. But we were emotionally peripheral instead of a truly committed, policy-shaping, calming and strengthening member. If we still don't embrace the advantages of current trading alliances, then surely Little England is well on the way to replacing Great Britain, as Scottish desire to break away will be strong. Little in every respect, we will be merely competitors with Europe. As for regaining influence in Europe and thereby the world, that, we must accept, is gone for now. However, I do believe that there will always be a way to regain lost ground, given understanding and the will of the people. Maybe though, some lessons will need to be learned again.

"Becoming competitors with Europe brings us back to the starting point of Sir Winston Churchill's speech. And remember, the population of all of Europe is only seven per cent of the world's population. On our own, we are indeed tiny."

There were no questions this time. Bill thought he had probably bored them to silence, when suddenly a new voice called out,

"What do you make of Boris Johnson then? You said you would talk about him"

"Okay," replied Bill, "just briefly though. He, like all our Prime Ministers, has far too much on his plate. Here is a man who has had to work out a policy with regard to the Covid-19 pandemic; he was in intensive care himself with it don't forget. He has a new relationship and a new baby. All the Brexit negotiations are going on now and he will have some big decisions to make very soon. We need a different system at the top of our government, whereby the leader of the party who becomes Prime Minister is automatically relieved of their role as party leader. The party simply elects a new leader. That would enable the Prime Minister to take a much broader view of every challenge and to be freed from party squabbles. They can form their cabinet from members of any party they want to. If we want men and women to be calm, considered and statesman-like in this role, then we must make it as manageable and as least stressful as possible. A Prime Minister who enjoys morning coffee, afternoon tea and finishes at 6pm barring emergencies, would appeal to me more than a stressed and harassed one. The decision to have a Brexit referendum by David Cameron is a prime example of a system which allows party issues to become confused with national interest. Remember, if it works, then leave it alone. If it doesn't work, then look for a change that will work. Parliament was accused of being unfit for service during the interminable Brexit debates. Has anything changed as a result? No, nothing is altered. We do need a change.

"As regards Boris Johnson personally, apart from wanting to make his day-to-day life easier, I enjoy his positivity, his optimism and his Billy Bunter style appeals to me. He has proved himself to be an effective leader who can take people with him. I happen to feel that the direction he is leading us in is dangerous and short-sighted, for the reasons I have given. He would have been a fabulous character within Europe but he has made his decision to get out.

"One of the bravest things a politician can do is to accept they were wrong and explain why. I don't expect that of Boris but I would have from the greats of history like Mandela and Gandhi. You never know, Boris might also prove himself to be great. He may even prove himself to be right.

Every one of us has a duty to think for ourselves and to make our own decisions. Not to decide is probably the most telling decision of all."

He paused, and then finished, "The problems with trade, Northern Ireland, and fishing rights will probably be settled eventually. The risk is of losing peace in Europe. It's about peace."

"Ladies, thank you all very much indeed."

The applause was enthusiastic. Bill felt it was for effort rather than substance but was pleased nonetheless.

AMELIA

The phone went early the following morning and Amelia's cheerful voice flooded down the line.,

"You have done it again Bill, everyone is talking about Brexit. My there are some strong opinions out there! I won't go so far as to say that any of those opinions have changed but they are certainly being aired!"

"Well, that's good," replied Bill. "And that's it for those talks now. I have lifted a weight off my chest, so it was good for me too. Now, how are you, Amelia? I bet you are running around like a mad thing. Your diary was brimming over."

"Yes, the diary does get out of hand sometimes. I keep it like that on purpose though. It's a long-term reaction to losing my husband, I think. That was one of those lifetime shocks that you never get over. The pain fades but the memory remains. I was well compensated financially, so that side of life is okay. It was the nature of his death that was so hard to accept. He was in Iraq but was killed in a stupid bloody accident when the helicopter he was in crashed without a shot being fired. I won't bore you with it all, perhaps one day but not now."

"That's fine Amelia. Just one question though, before we change the subject. Do you believe in life after death, or when we die do the lights just go out and that's it?"

"That's it I'm afraid. When we go, we go. That's maybe

why I do such a lot. It's a one-off show to me and I don't intend to waste it."

"You aren't wasting it, that's for sure. So, what are you up to today? Anything interesting?"

"I'm gardening this morning. This afternoon there is a fundraising meeting for the Air Ambulance and this evening, I am off to the cinema with two of my girlfriends. I can't even remember the film now but whatever it is, I love the escape of the cinema, especially with my gossipy friends. The cinema has only just re-opened, so we are sitting in little groups apparently. I will be damned glad when things come back to normal. Oh, and Alan is due home soon, so I am sorting out a few things for him. Do you fancy coming over when he gets back? He is interested in you I think and was asking after you."

"I would enjoy that very much. How about you two coming around to my place? Think about it and let me know. And send him my best wishes won't you."

"I will Bill. And our get-together date is in the diary as well."

Bill felt himself warm at her comment.

"That's great. Take care Miss Super Woman. Bye for now."

"Bye Bill. And thanks again for those talks."

The days passed pleasantly and Bill felt the weight of time on his hands. His home was small, so maintenance did not take long. He made a list of small projects to undertake, all of which he noted would take a little mental push to transfer from his note paper to reality. It read:

- Do a handstand (against a wall).
- Practice his unicycle skills — he had recently wobbled a distance of one hundred metres on a

unicycle to impress his grandchildren and now he wanted to be a little more reliable on it. He had achieved his initial success by practising in the back lane for ten minutes a day for six months. Apart from the bonus of getting to know his neighbours better, Bill had been genuinely pleased with his success. It had been captured on camera as proof! Quite good he thought, for he was sixty-nine years old at the time.

- Join the tennis club.
- Go kayaking.
- Learn some kind of musical instrument. This was a tricky one, as Bill was very unmusical and knew it.
- Write a book
- Take up running again… could he manage a half marathon?
- Go skiing. Bill's skiing prowess was minimal. He was sixty-eight before he had mastered the art of turning left on skis. Previously, his righthand turn had been slow but effective, to be followed by either a fall, or an ignominious slide off the piste when the inevitable left turn was required. Now he realised, he at last stood a chance of zig-zagging successfully down some gentle slopes.
- Brush up his German and French.

His list brought to mind his feelings of fatigue. He was definitely feeling better than he had been. Amelia had perked up his sex drive for sure. He sensed he was half better but to take life easy for a little longer would be wise.

"Getting the balance of life right is certainly a delicate business," he mused.

As his first move, he joined the tennis club and found himself enjoying both the company and gentle run around.

Amelia phoned to say that Alan wouldn't be back before their catch up but there was no other contact between them before their allotted day arrived.

Bill was his usual thoughtful self. He tucked his Cialis tablets into a pocket, wondering if he would need them or not. He took care to make himself clean and presentable. Into his pocket he slipped a bottle of massage oil. He had purchased it from the Body Shop. They hadn't used oil last time.

'You never know,' he thought.

As the weather was good, he set out on his bike in good time to slowly cycle the route. As he did so, he allowed the supremely agreeable sensation of being alive to flow through him. The autumnal breeze was flowing from behind, giving an effortless feel too his cycling. In his enhanced state of anticipation and buoyant mood, he found himself observing the vibrations from his handlebars passing through his hands and wrists to be absorbed somewhere within his forearms and elbows. He felt the clean coolness of the morning air passing through his nose, arriving effortlessly into his lungs. He enjoyed feeling the push of his quads flowing from one leg to the other, matching the rise and fall of each pedal in turn. His legs felt muscled, useful, ready for action. His attention was drawn to a thrush standing on the road ahead, with a snail in its beak about twenty yards away. He had spotted it beating the snail against the tarmac to break open the shell. As he rapidly approached, the bird had stopped the beating and carefully eyed the nearing machine and rider. Five yards ahead of arrival, the bird flew rapidly upwards to disappear behind the hedgerow, still gripping the snail. As Bill swooshed by, he was wondering if that had been a song thrush or a mistle thrush. He couldn't tell. It didn't matter. Either way, the cycle of life and death that was being displayed by the bird and snail filled him with a wonder of the nature of all things. It was such thoughts that had kept Bill calm amidst his own personal disasters and numerous medical crises. He was part of the world. He knew that and loved it. But he was not of it. Bill sensed that he was of something much bigger than the world here that was temporarily embracing him; and so was every living soul. His thoughts floated ahead to the woman who was waiting for him. He had noticed how clearly, she observed the life around her and how clearly she reacted to it. She was decisive, clear minded, totally honest, both to herself and the world around her.

'To thine own self be true,' he mused to himself.

A part of him was seriously analysing the way Amelia operated in life. It was simple and filled him with admiration. He sensed that she was offering him a chance to improve himself. He was feeling the need to raise his game as a human being.

He arrived a few minutes early but, before he had chance to knock on the door, it opened. There, with arms open, Amelia was to greet him.

They embraced tenderly before Amelia ushered him inside.

"I'll get some tea and then I want to hear what you have been up to. It's ages since I have seen you."

He sat in the same chair as before, feeling a mixture of excited anticipation and comfortableness, strangely combined.

He told Amelia about the tennis club, the people there and his list of planned activities. The unicycle made her laugh out loud.

"You'll never manage that, Bill!"

"I've already done the difficult bit," he protested. "The trick is learning that you don't ever need to fall off, you just step off. It's less painful that way."

"I'll need to see to believe," she declared.

Amelia went on to describe her own hectic life, the committees, the art society, the charities and she also described some of the walks she had undertaken. They were quite long walks, always taken alone.

"Sometimes I need time to reflect," she said. "I am not lonely, it's a necessary solitude."

They were quiet for a while, companionable in their silence, when Amelia spoke again.

"Bill, my bloody period started last night. I'm really sorry."

Bill sensed immediately that this was the end of his anticipated sexual romp with her. He was not a man that had any fear or dislike of menstrual flow and had in his time felt a primitive satisfaction looking down at his blood-stained genitals after sex at such a time. Women in general, he conceded, were usually not so inclined. Whether it was coyness or a hormonal thing, he couldn't tell.

"But," went on Amelia, "I could open up the back door for you."

It took Bill a brief moment to understand her, before he too laughed out loud.

"That, Amelia, would be absolutely wonderful!"

"I thought you might agree," she said, smiling at him.

Bill was not to know it but Amelia had been exasperated and frustrated when her period had started a few days earlier than normal. The idea of opening her 'back door' to him had come as a shock to her but had soon taken root as she was feeling safe with a gentle man. Her desire to explore sex again, many years after the loss of her husband, had already proved fun and enjoyable. In the true Tantric spirit, she was feeling happier, stronger and a new confidence was growing. Perhaps, she mused, she had more to offer the world than arranging talks for the Women's Institute, not that that was unimportant, came the afterthought.

They undressed in her bedroom again, feeling relaxed in each other's company and then with each other's nakedness.

He kissed her and their tongues slid together in intimate greeting. He felt his erection coming, much slower than the Cialis accelerated version but, somehow, just as satisfying.

Bill gently lifted his head away from hers and looked at her. He had already tousled her hair which now fell randomly around her shoulders. Her face held a quizzical smile. Her breasts beckoned him with their shape, weight and fall. The nipples protruded brown and strong, surrounded by their areolas of puckered skin. Her belly curved softly towards him and beneath that delicious curve lay the dark pubic hair that had fired him before. The erotic curtain of hair hid the secret mysterious world of her womanhood, which he had been so enraptured to enter.

With the lightest of pressure of his hands, Bill guided her to sit on the edge of the bed and then to rest on her back. He lifted her right shoulder and following his lead she rolled easily on to her front and lay there, relaxed, expectant, and happy.

Bill reached over to his trousers pocket and pulled out the massage oil. He had kept it close to himself to ensure it was warm. He opened the cap and filled the cupped palm of his hand with the oil and, tipping his hand, let it fall into the small of her back.

"Oooh, that's nice! Where did that come from, Mr Oily?"

"Body Shop's best," he answered.

He rubbed the oil around the small of her back in firm small circles which he gradually extended outwards. He enjoyed feeling the softness of her skin once more. The glistening texture of skin was enhanced by the glint of oily light from the myriad of tiny, silk-like hairs that lay flattened against her. Beneath this erotic covering, he could feel the firm shape of well-toned muscle. Gradually, he extended his hand pressures upwards to her upper back. When his fingers passed over her shoulder and passed inwards to squeeze the sides of her neck, she offered a groan of pleasure.

"That feels bloody marvellous. Don't stop or I'll kill you."

He didn't stop but slowly lowered his moving hands, delivering their slippery pressure across her upper back, her lower back and then her buttocks. He was gentle with the soft strong contours of her bottom and noticed her pelvis tilting in response to his touch but he did not linger there. Down the back of one thigh, then up the inside of it. He briefly let his hand pass close enough to her crutch to brush the underside of her hair and then passed down the back of the other thigh. Her knees and lower legs and finally her feet were all in turn squeezed, oiled and caressed.

Realising he had forgotten her arms, Bill returned first to her shoulders and then gently squeezed and kneaded his way down to her hands, giving each arm in turn, full measure of caressing attention. He pressed gently on her palms and followed with a leisurely oily sliding grip around her thumbs and fingers one by one. Bill achieved a feeling of intimacy matching the touch of any erotic zone.

"Thank you, Bill," she murmured.

Bill returned to her buttocks and dripped oil onto her already shining curves. This time, instead of slowly increasing the width of his circular hand movements he slowly decreased the size of each sweep, circling slowly around her anus. With his free hand he pulled one buttock gently sideways to reveal her perfect rosetta. Gently he brought his thumb to the very centre of it, pressed gently upon it and waited.

"Are you okay" he asked.

"Yes."

He pushed inwards, his thumb slid inwards half an inch. She gasped but remained still. He felt the pressure of her anus around the end of his thumb. He pushed inwards again, slowly and suddenly his thumb passed through the muscle resistance and entered the soft, dark warmth of her body. She remained absolutely still. Bill turned his hand slightly and allowed his index finger to run along the base of her buttock cleavage, and rocked his thumb back and forth inside her.

"Still okay?"

"Yes."

Bill gently removed his thumb, then placed himself astride her looking at her shining back and the curving bottom beneath him. His attention to her had been absolute and his erection, which had originally become fully developed, had now partly softened. He wrapped his fingers around himself and gave himself some stimulation, soaking in the sight before him to boost the effect. When happy with his state, Bill then tipped oil over himself and dropped a liberal amount around her anus, before lowering himself on to her. By propping himself up on one elbow and using his free hand to direct his penis, Bill was able to apply pressure from himself directly on to her. First, he slipped upwards, then he slipped downwards, then he felt the pressure hold and he pushed inwards. The blunt head of him entered her a little. She gasped.

"Okay?"

"Yes."

He pushed again and she gasped once more. He didn't speak this time, he sensed she was busy within herself, accepting a little pain, wanting to experience it. He pushed again, and suddenly the head of his penis was inside her and he felt the grip of her anus holding him there.

"Oooh," she breathed.

Bill remained still for a moment longer and then pushed again. This time the glistening shaft of his penis passed easily through her, until his passage into her body was stopped as his pubic hair flattened against her buttocks. Gently he removed his elbow from beside her and lowered himself onto her.

On her face was a half-smile. Her eyes were open, gazing sightlessly at her pillow, her lips were open.

"Is that nice?" Bill asked.

A tiny nod of the head in response was all he needed.

They lay so combined for fifteen minutes. Bill didn't thrust at all. Occasional movements came from her when she squeezed Bill's penis with her anus, making him gasp and her laugh.

After that time his erection started to fade, and he felt a gradual withdrawal happening which accelerated as it progressed until he was expelled from her with a rapid slithering sensation that prompted a little exclamation from them both. Both of them were feeling a sense of exultation.

Neither of them had had an orgasm. They lay side by side and sleep enveloped them both.

It was Amelia who opened her eyes first and after a few minutes lying still beside him, she poked him back to life.

"Bill, I want you to do me a favour"

"What's that then?"

"I want to see you masturbate. Over me. Do you mind?"

Bill didn't mind, especially as the quietness of their anal meeting had left him with a tense ache. Amelia rolled onto her back and he passed a leg over her to sit upon her. The sensation of her soft abdomen beneath his buttocks was both novel and stimulating. Below him he saw her breasts falling away, curved, heavy and delicious. Her face was framed by unruly hair, her mouth was laughing, naughty and happy. He reached down and felt the weight of her right breast and with his free hand started to rub himself in a practised and familiar way. As his own arousal mounted, he gripped her body more strongly between his thighs. His hand on her breast found her nipple and as he squeezed her there, her own hands lifted to him, raising up her breasts towards him, as with finger and thumb she gripped both of his nipples. Remembering how he had reacted to this last time, Amelia pulled him hard, very hard. The rapturous sensation that shot through Bill connected to his penis and his rubbing on himself became feverish as the painful pleasure fired through him. He felt the irresistible coming of his end. His thighs gripped her body ever more tightly. He rose up and cried out as drops of semen dropped on to her chest, her neck and face.

He sank down onto her, head bowed.

The prolonged period of silence that followed was eventually broken by Amelia.

"Wow," she said, "that was fun!"

Bill smiled, kissed her on the lips and flopped down beside her.

"You're quite remarkable for your age Bill," she commented.

"I'm lucky I think," said Bill. "I don't have any health problems and don't need any tablets, except of course the occasional Cialis."

"Did you use them today?"

"No but they are in my pocket, just in case."

"Well, they can stay there for now. I'm going to get us a snack. You, my man, can lay there and rest on your laurels. You have made me feel really good Bill. I mean that."

To Bill, such a compliment was the best he could ever hope for. Were he to die today, he knew he would die a happy man. But beneath such thoughts, Bill felt a certainty that he was not going to die today. He had things to do in life yet and he would be meeting his destiny whatever it was. Such thoughts just came to him and were suddenly accompanied by the unasked-for knowledge that, not only was his destiny far from here, it had nothing to do with Amelia.

Sitting naked in bed together, in the companionable zone that successful lovers fall to, they sipped tea and ate chocolate biscuits.

"Bill?"

"Yes Amelia." Bill looked at her with a smile, as clearly a pre-thought-out question was being framed.

"You know you once asked me if I believed in life after death and I said 'No'. Well now can you tell me what you think?"

"Okay. You are in the mood then?"

“Yes”

Bill set off. “Well, I think yes, there is life after death. But nobody actually knows. That’s why I like talking about it really, because no one is going to win or lose an argument about it. The best minds in the world haven’t taken us forward a millimetre.”

“Lots of people say they know though.”

“For sure they do. I am one of them I guess, because if you believe in something strongly enough, it feels like knowledge. But you can’t prove it. It has to be an act of faith.”

“Well, why do you believe there is life after death if there is no proof?”

“If there was proof, it would destroy all our freedom to behave just as we think fit, like we do now. We are free to do good or bad. Think how our mindset would change if we knew, I mean REALLY knew, that after death we carried on?”

“But you say that you do.”

“Well, I believe that we do. That doesn’t make me one jot better than someone like you, who doesn’t agree. You are just a bundle of molecules, are you not?”

“I suppose I am.”

“Well, you are a very lovely bundle of molecules, Amelia” He laughed. “It just doesn’t matter. What does matter is if you are a decent person. Are you generous, honest and nice to meet? Do you mean well towards other people, or ill? Are your thoughts kind, or malign? That’s what this life is all about. What is important is really simple and understandable to just about anybody. You don’t need a degree in Theology.”

“Are you a good person then?”

“I’m a selfish old git.” he replied, looking directly at her.

“Well, you’re not a bad selfish old git then” It was her turn to laugh at him.

"Why," she asked, "why do you believe in something you can't prove so, so, how shall I say, devoutly?"

"That's simple enough. I am persuaded by the beauty and order of nature. Scientists are revealing more and more of the wonders that make life work. It is all so mind boggling that I find myself having to stop thinking about it. I have to get my feet back on the ground by having a cup of tea or doing something practical. I don't believe that the bundle of molecules that actually is your body could have happened by random chance. You and all the rest of us and everything else for that matter, are just too wonderful. They are to me anyway."

"So, you don't believe in Darwin's theory of evolution then."

"I do actually. We can see that in action. But beneath it there must be another deeper process, more spiritual if you like, guiding things along. I don't think you and I are sat here talking about it by chance. There is something hidden and wonderful at work."

"I can't agree with you, Bill. When the helicopter crash killed my husband and three others with him, the engine failure was as random as anything can be. No, you have to be wrong Bill. He should still be here."

The sudden seriousness entering the conversation made Bill think carefully as to what he said next.

"He is here in one sense. What's his name, Amelia?"

"Hugo. He was a tough nut. He was made for the military. Alan and he were often in the same squad. They usually worked in teams of four. He was only flying to a briefing when they crashed, in perfect conditions apparently."

Her pain was still there.

"There is no way that we can make sense of life here on earth as we see it." Bill replied. "There is pain, disease, death and tragedy all mixed up with the best of life. Often it seems desperately unfair. What is the point of having a stillborn baby, for example, or a hopelessly damaged one? Who invented a disease like malaria? God? So much doesn't make sense to us. Every awful occurrence will be a challenge for someone to respond to. Anyway Amelia, here is how I believe the whole show rolls. I say believe, mind you, because remember I don't know any more than you do. And I don't tell many people what I am saying to you either. They would probably send around the men in white coats to drag me off!"

"Go on then, Mr Confucius"

"Well first, I have never really liked the term God. I don't suspect a single, all-knowing figure is out there watching us. My concept of God is of the entire universe, and all the energy in it. Everything around us, as well as our own bodies, is a form of energy. Even a block of concrete is a mass of spinning particles full of energy. We are not separate from the universe, we are all part of it. We people are all part of the same thing. The special energy of life is what we are all about and it gives us experiences that a block of concrete won't have, like a sense of good and bad, love and hate. Our world is a place of experience. Here we can experience whatever we want to create in response to our lives, because the opposite is here to create the experience. You can't experience hotness unless there is coldness. So, if you want the experience of being a teacher, you need to go where there is ignorance. If you want to be a healer, you go where there is disease. If you want the experience of courage, you must go where there is something to scare you. This is often summarised by saying, if you want the experience of being a light, you have to go into the darkness. This world offers the dramas of life which enable us to experience all these things. Here, on earth, this is our darkness, so we have a chance to experience ourselves shining. When life here ends, say when Hugo died in the helicopter crash, the whole thing seems like a meaningless flash in the pan. But if his life, and every other life, is one of many lives that take us on a series of journeys, then it is possible to start to make sense of the randomness of whatever we are experiencing now."

"Are you saying you believe in reincarnation?"

"Absolutely I am. Not just a few times but as many lives as you choose, until you have really explored what this world has to offer."

"So what happens then, where do you go to when you die?"

"Back to the spiritual world of blissfulness that you came from. And there you stay, until you decide to come and have another adventure here on earth."

"Oh, bollocks Bill. Where did you dream this up from?"

"Well, I had these ideas half formed in my head. Then I did some reading and found that others had already put into words what I was half thinking anyway. There's loads written about it but I found one particular book where it is all described far better than I am able to tell you now."

"You had better tell me the name of the book. I suppose I had better read it. But don't expect me to be a convert."

"Fine, but I don't want or need you to be a convert Amelia. You only need read a few pages and that will be enough to tell you if the book is for you, or not. I'm quite happy to accept you as the bundle of randomly assembled of molecules that you are. The block of concrete is a bundle of molecules as well. What we are talking about is the difference between you or me and the block of concrete. Your body is more amazing than the concrete, with all the things it can do. Your brain allows you to think and feel things like hope and love. Concrete can't do that. And also, there is a hidden guiding part of you, the eternal bit; your soul. Concrete won't have that either. Your soul gives you insights and messages which you need to tune into, to take advantage of. Your soul is never afraid, because it is a part of the universe that is eternal and it is our hidden guide during all of our lives."

"Oh, I don't know," said Amelia wistfully. "And coming back time after time sounds quite exhausting."

"Coming back isn't a random thing. You have eternal spiritual companions. For you, Hugo will be one of them. Together with these companions you work out what form of life on earth will suit your next spiritual journey. So, the time in history you are born into, where you are born and the type of family set up you are born into, doesn't happen by chance."

"Pull the other one Bill! I'm not really getting this."

"There's nothing to get Amelia. The only thing that matters is how you live your life now. You have the huge challenge of creating a good life, one that you will be proud of, without Hugo. You could become a life changer for others going through the same thing. That is important. The rest is up to dreamers like me. But I do dream, because these ideas give a rationale to life which fits in with the order of the universe. Brief lives which twinkle and go out just don't make sense. The other thing I like about these ideas is that it gives some explanation about evil people, bad people who cause so much pain. Without them, the world couldn't offer us all the challenges it does. Without Hitler for example, Britain would never have had the challenge there to confront. In his way, Hitler was as important as Churchill. You can't experience goodness unless badness exists. The two usually balance and they are as important as each other. At the end of the day, Hitler went to heaven."

"God help us in heaven then."

"You know the song, All things Bright and Beautiful?"

"Of course I do."

"Well, in my mind it's only half right. God, or the universe, created everything, including the shitty bits. The shitty bits enable us to experience the good bits."

"This is all fantasy, Bill."

Undeterred Bill pressed on.

"When we leave this earth, or in other words, when we die, we go back to the spiritual world where everything is bright and beautiful. There we stay until we want another chance to glow in the dark."

"Have you a scrap of proof about any of this?"

"Of course not. And what's more, it is a waste of time looking for it. You can feel it though, if you want to. If you don't want to, it doesn't matter. But one thing is for sure, you'll never work it out."

"Have you finished?"

"Yes."

"Pass the phone then, what's the number for the white coat brigade?"

Bill smiled happily at her.

Amelia dismissed his talk, feeling an underlying irritation about it. But that night, as she pulled her covers around her, she allowed a small pleasure to creep into her mind. Somebody thought that Hugo existed still and she liked that thought.

Alan returned from another mysterious mission and by phone, it was agreed that Amelia and Alan would meet with Bill at the local garden centre café. There they would arrange a lunch date which Bill was happy to cater for.

The garden centre was four miles out of town and Bill set off happily on his bike. The initial part of the ride saw him raptly alert as the vehicles around him jostled like dodgem cars. The Cornish holiday season had ended now but local traffic seemed ever busier now the lockdown was easing. A mile down the road, a turn off led him onto a quiet route which then led all the way to the back gates of the garden centre. During the initial hectic part of his ride, Bill had been passed by a slouched and pimply youth, who was skateboarding at noisy speed down the road, attending to his mobile phone as he went. Bill felt the tutt tutt of adult common sense, mixing awkwardly with outright awe at the lad's skill and confidence. Youth was and is, a wonderful and mysterious thing he mused, as he pedalled slowly up a leaf-strewn slope. The breeze was fresh. Autumn had thrown down her mantle to nature and time would soon be up. 'That's where I am, Autumn.' He thought, 'What's left?'

Alan looked very well and Amelia was fussing around him in a way that Bill found entrancing and a little puzzling. There was no need to pamper this tough looking man.

Tea, all white and none with sugar, was delivered in solid and generous-sized mugs, each adorned by pictures of mice. Bill started the conversation,

"Had a good trip away then Alan?"

"Extremely good, thank you Bill. I was very pleased by that, because it was also my last tour of duty. My time is up in the army now. I could have stayed on but the pension is good enough for me now. More importantly, one of my best mates and I plan to start a business together. We worked out that, if we both put in about half of our lump sum termination pay, we will have enough to get our little dream going."

"Wow!" said Bill. "Big changes then."

"We want to run an activity centre for youngsters. There's a disused quarry just out of town and we plan to put some jumps and slides around it and create a fun outdoor leisure centre. We want it for youngsters though. It will be fun, with a bit of daring thrown in."

Bill thought of the young skateboarder.

"So you'll be staying local then. In your home with Amelia?"

Before he could answer, Amelia broke in. "I might be selling my half to Alan. Not quite decided yet."

"Are you thinking of moving away?"

"Oh no" she replied carelessly, "I'll still be around."

Bill sensed it best to leave her to tell him whatever she wanted to, rather than to offer up his own questions. As it was, she gave no more away and the subject soon turned to the lunch that Bill was going to deliver.

"Do you like Cornish pasties?" Bill enquired. "That would be a bit different."

"You bet," replied Alan, whilst Amelia signalled affirmatively with enthusiastic nodding of her head.

"Tell you what then," said Bill, "they will take an hour to cook, so I'll put them in the oven and then we will have an hour for a drink at the Red Lion. So long as we get back on time, they will be just ready as we come through the door."

"A cracking plan," declared Alan and he and Bill exchanged a smacking high five.

The day was agreed, only two days hence and the rendezvous in the pub was militarily scheduled for 12.00 hours.

The conversation drifted a little aimlessly after that and soon, they bade each other farewell and Bill was back on his bike, with Cornish pasties being his latest single-minded focus.

That mental focus faded well before he reached the busy main road. As his tyres scrunched over fallen leaves, he found himself wondering why Amelia had suddenly changed her mind about selling her half of her childhood home to Alan. 'A bit odd,' he thought, inconclusively. He had hoped that another get-together date would have been arranged but somehow, Amelia seemed distracted. With Alan there, Bill hadn't been able to ask directly.

The supermarket he passed on the way home was a Sainsbury's, which provided easy access to the pasty ingredients. Parking his bicycle, he explored the aisles. Generally, Bill had a preference for Lidl or Aldi, where the simplicity of transaction appealed to him. You chose what you wanted and paid for it without the fuss of coupons, petrol vouchers or loyalty cards. All of such things merely increased prices elsewhere in the store and Bill couldn't see the point. He soon found the required swede, onion, potato, beef skirt and puff pastry, which he purchased, managing not to wince when politely asked if he had a Nectar card. He loaded everything into his rucksack, together with a few cans of lager, which he thought Alan might appreciate. He had some wine of every hue already at home. For himself, he would indulge in his recently acquired liking of alcohol-free beer, Bavaria being his current favourite. He knew that the true Cornish pasty makers would probably scoff at him for using puff pastry. They would hand make shortcrust pastry. Bill was no purist and he liked the purchased puff stuff.

The required two days after the garden centre meeting soon passed and Bill set to work making the pasties. He reckoned it would take him an hour to prepare them. Smiling to himself as he started with military promptness at 11.00 hours, he set to work. First the meat was cleaned of fibrous tissue and most of the fat and cut into small pieces. Bill planned to make four pasties and freeze one of them, as a handy treat for another day. The puff pastry came in a block which cut neatly into four. He rolled out each thick slice of it over a layer of plain flour into the required dinner plate sized circle. He diced an onion into small pieces, then the swede, and finally the potato. Potato was always the first to discolour when exposed to air, so he habitually cut it up last.

Bill didn't often cook but, when he did, he made a point of doing it in an enjoyable fashion. As he worked, he took sips from a glass of sherry and, in the background, music tracks floated through the house from his collection of CDs.

He took the discs of rolled out pastry one by one. He slid the rolling pin under the far half of the pastry circle and dropped the diced potato onto the nearside flat half. On top of the potato went the meat, which he seasoned with salt and pepper. Then came the diced onions and finally the swede. He placed a small knob of butter on top of each half of the heaped ingredients, before moistening the puff pastry edges by brushing them with water. He lifted the front and back edges of the pastry together and pinched them closed with his fingers. Then he worked his way along the stuck edges, folding them over and over in the time-honoured manner of crimping. A brief stab in the pastry casing, to allow steam to escape finished the job. Bill liked to add the extra ingredient of love to his pasties.

He was feeling some satisfaction in finishing the fourth one, when at that very moment the phone went. It was Amelia.

"Hi Bill, how are you?"

"I'm good thanks Amelia, just finishing the pasties."

"That's why I'm phoning. Is there time for you to do an extra one? If not, I can always share one with Alan. But Alan's friend who he wants to set up the adventure business with is here and it would be nice if he could come along. He's a really super guy."

"No problem at all. I made four anyway. They will be going in the oven on time and I'll be down the pub about ten minutes after. See you then. Oh, by the way, what's Alan's mate called?"

"He's called Michael."

"Okay. See you soon."

There was absolutely nothing in the call to indicate it but Bill wondered instinctively, if Michael might mean a lot more to Amelia than being Alan's prospective business partner. Her description of him as a really super guy had been delivered with great enthusiasm, a passion even. He felt his insides flip a bit. He had learned to trust his instincts more and more. He had already sensed that Amelia and he were never going to be the sought-after, 'one couple against the world' unit, that so many humans yearn for. She had never wanted to share her social life with him. Perhaps also, somewhere deeper inside, he knew that his future required him to be emotionally free. Why, he couldn't say.

"Shit," he said quietly to himself. He slid the pasties into the pre-heated oven, took off his flour-covered apron and headed off for the meet up in the pub.

If there was a match for Alan's tough look, then Michael had it, although his actual appearance was markedly different. He was a tad taller, slimmer but his movement was panther like in ease. His face was lined in a way that somehow suggested experiences beyond the ken of most men. His skin was tanned, his hair unblemished black. He spoke in a gentle way, making a caressing, quiet sound and what he said was enhanced by his readiness to smile.

Bill warmed to him instantly.

Amelia, beside him, was being very attentive. She was super alert. She watched the unspoken assessment going on between the men and seeing the goodwill emanating from Bill, she felt relaxation easing her tension and a warm glow of pride in him. He was conducting himself with an endearing charm. She had been a little nervous of this moment as the two men were both important to her in very different ways. Much of Amelia's success in life had come from an ability to clearly see what was being presented to her and to make a decision based on whatever that was. She never complicated an issue with thoughts of what she would have liked something to be. She was possessed of a natural self-honesty, which responded to reality in life rather than dreams of wishful thinking. This had translated into an effortless honesty in her dealings with the world around her. In a word, she had integrity. She used tact and guile to make her case in any situation, her firmness being delivered with a gentle touch. Most of those with whom she had had disagreements had remained friends or supportive colleagues. The few whom she failed to satisfy, soon dropped out of her life once they had realised that her mind had no place for them in it. Bill had proved to be an unexpectedly good lover and she had even come to enjoy his dreamy and usually impractical ideas. She could gladly have embarked on further amorous sessions with him. But now life had presented her with a completely different prospect, in the darkly handsome form of Michael. Here was someone she felt instantly proud to walk beside. When he held her hand, her spirit soared. When he kissed her, she was his. She knew instinctively where her future lay. Her mind was exercised merely in the best and kindest manner to let Bill know.

For his part, Bill had taken on board that his meeting with Michael seemed to be very important for Amelia, who was clearly watching them intently.

"Pleased to meet you Michael," said Bill, who then carried on boldly asking, "and what can I get you sir?"

"We are doing the buying Bill." It was Alan speaking now. "You have been busy making us all pasties. That's worth several pints in my book!"

"Afternoon gents."

Martin had strolled up to them, giving a brief nod to Michael as he did so, recognising the stranger in their midst.

"Hi Martin," said Bill. "You know Amelia from the WI, I think. This is her brother Alan, who saved my bacon a few months ago, you remember; and this is his mate and business partner to be, Michael."

Martin leaned towards Alan and Michael in a conspiratorial way. It pleased Bill to observe that Martin was now looking fit. His trousers laid comfortably on him, his complexion was fresh. The drunken youth who had squeezed his neck had clearly done him a favour.

"Mr Alan and Mr Michael, let me warn you now, you are in dangerous company sharing your time and good beer with this man." He twitched towards Bill. "He runneth over with crazy ideas and is, as a rule, well worth staying away from."

Amelia burst out in a release of laughter.

"You know him don't you!" she exclaimed "He is full of strange ideas, you are right. But I love you like that Bill," she said, looking at him. "Please don't change, whatever that nasty man says!"

Martin raised his eyebrows, stood upright and said simply,

"Gentlemen, what can I bring you?"

They found seats near a window, which lent a view of tossing branches and whirling leaves dancing around in the wind. They all had a drink to enjoy and the atmosphere within their cosy circle was enhanced by the warmth of the pub, which securely sheltered them from the autumnal gusts beyond. Across the room flames flickered and sparked around freshly stacked logs. The atmosphere brought to Bill's mind his favourite German word:

"Gemütlich" he whispered to Amelia. He was mightily surprised when she responded without hesitation, also in German with a perfect accent, "Du hast Recht."

Placing his glass on the table, Michael turned to Bill and asked,

"Have you been winding him up then, Bill?"

"I seem to wind everybody up," replied Bill, "often by mistake! I was having a go at Martin about our political system the other day, that's probably what's on his mind. He'll have me down as some sort of treasonous schemer for sure."

"Does the government displease you then?"

"You bet it does. They say one thing, then do another."

Amelia braced herself for a lecture on Brexit, which she didn't want to happen because both Alan and Michael were strongly in favour of it, as most military people she knew seemed to be. Somewhat to her relief, Bill started off on a new tack — the environment.

"For example, we hear from the government that they will do all they can to protect the environment. Next thing, they give the nod to a third runway at Heathrow. I know that's actually held up by environmental concerns at the moment and quite right too but, before that, they were nodding it through. How does that add up? And then there's HS 2. Did you know that right now, the train time from Manchester to London is only just over two and a half hours as it is. How does smashing through middle England countryside, destroying fields and ancient woodlands square with caring for the environment? It's balderdash. They want to reduce the journey time to just over an hour. What's the mighty rush all about? Now if just half of that ludicrous amount of money was put into building decent cycleways around the whole land, in each and every city, then now you're talking. We'd have something that would actually make ordinary lives better.

"I'm not particularly against this government Michael. I'm aggravated by every government that doesn't clearly define its aim as being to improve the well-being of its citizens. That is quite different to seeking endless growth, especially when the whole world knows that such an aim is not sustainable."

"Wow," replied Michael and gave a deep relaxed laugh.

"I see what our Martin means!"

Bill smiled comfortably back, feeling better for having released some more of his pent-up feelings. He felt Amelia's fingers briefly find and squeeze his, under the table.

Their conversation ambled over lighter matters and very soon, it was time to return to Bill's small home in time to catch the pasties at their best. Alan and Michael walked along in front of Amelia and Bill. As they neared Bill's home, Michael gave Alan a hearty slap on his muscular back. It was a friendly slap, Bill knew. However, had it landed on his own back and impacted on his muscle denuded scapulae, it would have just about knocked him over.

'They are real men's men,' Bill thought to himself. He saw how a confident and robust Amelia would fit in well with them. It was a world she knew of old as well. Nothing clear had been said but Bill was slowly realising that Amelia was besotted with Michael and her feelings for himself had been reduced to those of concern.

As they reached his home, he turned to her solemn face, and smiled.

"Don't worry Amelia, it's all right. I know."

THE NEXT CHAPTER

The days were passing pleasantly enough. Bill found the tennis club enjoyable, his cycle rides fun and his enjoyment of evening television excellent. His energy levels were returning, though his desire to return to any form of medicine had now reduced itself to extinction. Throughout it all though, was the void. There was no call from Amelia to anticipate, no WI talk for her to be appalled by and no get-together with her to look forward to. He felt stupid to be so forlorn at his age, when such voids, such pains, were only supposed to reside within the tortuous realms of the agonies of youth. Michael had appeared out of the blue and Amelia had, it seemed, instantly fallen for him. He was sure of that. He knew that the two of them looked a perfect match in a way that he and Amelia could never be.

Still, he told himself, he had always found himself attracted to women of his own age. They always offered a comfort of shared experience that was bonding and to Bill, very important. Some of them still looked ridiculously pretty, in their seventies. He had nothing at all against partnerships or marriages of people of wildly varying ages — but that was not the natural inclination for him. Perhaps this was all just as well.

Despite his selfless justifications of the situation, Bill felt disappointed and sad.

Two weeks after the pasty dinner, her letter dropped onto

his doormat.

'Dear Bill,' it read.

'I don't know how you realised so soon that I was in love with Michael but I am, and it is turning into something very special. It is the first time since Hugo was killed that I can feel myself ready to relate fully to another human being, with all the intensity and enhancement that it brings to everyday life. Sometimes, I feel a bit like you, that something divine is at work. Being me, I dismiss it but maybe you have sown a seed! Alan is buying me out of our old house, so Michael and I can buy one of our own. I am so excited by a new place we have found. It feels like the opening up of a new chapter. I don't feel the need to run around and organise other people any more. Your WI talks seem to be the swansong for us both. I still get people going on to me about them, you old stirrer you!

What you have given me Bill may sound strange. I saw you liking me and then enjoying me. The effect on my self-esteem was huge. I am not too self-deprecating to know that as looks go, I have been lucky. But the most beautiful woman in the world is wasted unless she finds someone that sees that in her. I could see you watch me in that way and you did it without making me feeling awkward, which was quite clever of you really. Then, you listened to what I had learned on those Tantra weekends and you actually understood what I said. We were warned on the courses not to try and explain it to people in general, because a harsh and painful judgement can come flying back at you. Judgements like that help no one but are often thrown by people who are probably just disappointed in their own lives. Anyway, you had no judgement and then you surprised me and then you thrilled me. You really are a dark horse, Bill!

I bless you and wish you well on your own journey. You have set me up for my next chapter, with a renewed confidence that has washed away memories of unhappy times. Michael is a supremely, wonderful man and I feel I am a woman fit to be at his side. He is just as besotted with me as you were. There is something appealingly childlike about you men and I wouldn't want it any other way.

Don't change Bill. Do your special maverick thing in life. I will be watching!

This letter is a goodbye to a chapter in both our lives and also a welcome to the next one.

Michael and I are building our home and life together. You will always be a special and honoured guest in our journey and should you ever wish, I would, in turn, feel supremely honoured to share in parts of yours.

With my love,

Amelia XX

Bill sat at his table and read through the letter a second time. He felt tears pricking his eyes. For five contemplative minutes he sat motionless. Then Amelia's own words came from his lips.

"Fuck me," he declared.

And then his own words came.

"It's time to take Maisie on that run."

His energy had returned.